Kissed by Fire

Also by Shéa MacLeod

Kissed by Darkness

Kissed by Fire

The Sunwalker Saga, Book Two

Shéa MacLeod

Montlake
Romance

First edition © 2011 Shéa MacLeod
Montlake edition © 2012

Published by Montlake Romance
P.O. Box 400818
Las Vegas, NV 89140

ISBN-13: 9781612185637
ISBN-10: 1612185630

For Elizabeth
on her birthday

Prologue

"Jack, would you get off the damn floor? This is ridiculous."

Not to mention embarrassing. Nothing like having the guy you just got jiggy with kneeling half-naked on the floor while you lounge completely naked on the couch. It's definitely not as sexy as you might think.

He didn't move.

"Fine, I command you. Get your ass off the floor."

He did, but he remained at some sort of parade attention with his right arm crossed over his chest, fist against his heart.

Was he kidding?

One minute everything had been fine. Great, even. We'd just had some of the hottest sex of my life, for crying out loud. The next I'd touched that stupid Atlantean amulet we'd finally gotten back from the psychopath who stole it, and the room lit up like a blue Christmas tree. Even worse, Jack—the macho former Templar Knight—had gone from rocking my world to throwing himself to his knees to profess his undying duty and honor, or whatever knights do.

"Jack, this is ridiculous..." Irritation boiled through me. I wasn't full-out angry yet, but I was getting there.

"This is serious, Morgan. You are a member of the royal bloodline of Atlantis. You activated the Heart." He nodded toward the amulet, which I'd ever so gracefully dropped on the living room rug. "Right now you are the most important person on this planet. It is my duty to protect you."

I frowned. I was pretty sure he was exaggerating about being the most important person. It just sounded ridiculous. This whole Atlantis thing was driving me nuts.

Apparently, not only had Atlantis been a real place, but I am a freaking Atlantean princess. Well, member of the royal bloodline, anyway. And I am supposed to bond with the amulet and...Well, nobody knows. Save the world, maybe. Which is, frankly, nuts.

Killing vampires I understand. I am a hunter, after all. It's my job. This? Not so much. I decided to change tack.

I patted the couch beside me. "Why don't you come over here? I think we were right in the middle of something." OK, so I'm not exactly brilliant at the seduction, but we'd just had mind-blowing sex, for goodness' sake. I figured it was a foregone conclusion he'd want to take up where we'd left off.

Boy, was I wrong.

Jack shook his head. "I think you should go, Morgan."

I blinked. "Excuse me?"

"I am your guardian. You are a royal. There can be nothing between us other than that." He stood ramrod straight, face utterly impassive.

"Jack..."

"I'll let you get dressed." He turned and strode from the room. I stared after him in utter confusion. Somewhere in the back of the house a door slammed with finality.

For the rest of the week, I called, I texted, and I banged on his front door until I had bruises and the neighbors started giving me funny looks, but Jack refused to talk to me. So I finally did what I do best: I hunted him down and cornered him. I actually broke into his house and waited for him to come home one night. Yeah, totally stalker, but it was the only way I was going to get him to talk.

It wasn't me who started something between us in the first place. I'd never dreamed that a simple job to hunt down a sunwalker and recover a stolen heirloom would result in finding someone I thought I could share my life with. But once Jack and I joined forces to find the amulet that started this ridiculous princess of Atlantis business, it was clear there was something between us. Something important. Something I wasn't going to let go quite so easily.

So I sat there on the sofa in the dark just waiting for him to come home. The minute he entered the room and switched the light on, I pounced.

"Listen, Jack, this is bullshit. You've got to talk to me. What the hell is going on?"

He didn't even blink. If he was surprised, he sure didn't show it. "My lady…"

"Don't you 'my lady' me," I snarled, poking my finger into his chest. It was very satisfying poking a man nearly twice my size—and an ancient, immortal Templar Knight, to boot. "I am tired of this crap. One minute we're all hot and heavy, and the next minute you're bowing and scraping and acting like I've got rabies or something."

He didn't even crack a smile. Which isn't that unusual, actually. Jack isn't exactly expressive even in the best of times. That sounds all romantic and shit, like a proper Mr. Darcy, but in real life, it is annoying as hell.

He heaved a sigh. "Listen, Morgan." He plopped down onto his chocolate chenille sofa, so I curled into the overstuffed matching chair opposite him. Jack had the comfiest living room furniture ever. "Things have changed. When I thought you were just another one of us…" He waved his hand around as though trying to grasp inspiration from the ether.

One of us. I knew what he meant. He meant sunwalkers. Humans with Atlantean DNA who'd been infected by vampirism. The Atlantean DNA forces the sickness to mutate so that, instead of becoming vampires, they became powerful, nearly immortal creatures who can walk in the sun. Jack seems to think I am one of them. Frankly, I think he is bloody nuts. At least, I hope he is.

"So, what, you can date another sunwalker, but not me?" I knew he'd had lovers before me, plenty of them, and I couldn't help it if my voice was just this side of plaintive. I had a sudden flashback to Alex, my ex-fiancé. But Alex had said he never loved me. I am convinced Jack still does. Somehow, I think that hurts even more.

"I'm the guardian, Morgan."

"Yeah, of the amulet. And the amulet found its owner, so you can stop worrying about the stupid thing. It's my problem now." As the last of the royal bloodline, the amulet had bonded to me.

Well, sort of. Technically, it was supposed to download all the knowledge and power of ancient Atlantis into my brain. Only, that hadn't happened. Not as far as I can tell, anyway. Possibly, it has something to do with waking the darkness in me, which, believe me, is freaking scary, but otherwise, everything is still normal. Normal for me, anyway. What I do know is that, essentially, the amulet is mine.

He smiled a little. "That's true. The amulet is now yours to protect, but the guardian's job doesn't end with the amulet. It merely transfers to the one who holds it."

I blinked a little. "Say what?" Call me slow, but I didn't like where this was heading.

"I am now *your* guardian, Morgan Bailey. It is my sworn duty to protect you, Key of Atlantis, Keeper of the Heart."

Oh, bloody hell. I now have my own personal bodyguard. Fantastic.

I narrowed my eyelids. "So, why'd I have to hunt you down, then?"

"Just because you can't see me doesn't mean I'm not there."

"Right, OK," I said with a nod, trying to be all reasonable. "I'm the keeper. You're the guardian. Fine. I still don't see the problem."

His features were drawn and tight, and he looked more tired than I'd ever seen him, his ocean-colored eyes shadowed, golden skin paler than usual. The delicate skin under his eyes was so deeply purple it looked like a bruise. Frankly, he looked like crap.

"The problem is that if I get involved with you...romantically, I can't do my job. That is why the guardian is forbidden to have a...relationship with the keeper."

"Oh, that is bullshit," I snapped, both infuriated and hurt. I wasn't sure which emotion was stronger at the moment. "That's some stupid, crappy rule from, what, ten thousand years ago? This is the twenty-first century, for crying out loud."

"And the logic still applies." His voice was firm. "If a warrior grows too close to his charge, it becomes impossible for him to execute his duty." He sounded like he was quoting from a rule book. He probably was. *Dos and Don'ts for the Single Templar.*

"So get someone else to play guardian. You can be, like...the assistant guardian or something."

"I can't, Morgan. The amulet chose me. There's nothing I can do to change that. I wouldn't even if I could."

There really hadn't been much to say after that. He wasn't budging and neither was I. I'd thought I'd finally found someone to love. Someone who'd love me back just as much. Someone I could depend on. Losing that...It made my heart hurt. But you can't force someone to want to be with you, and short of smacking him upside the head with a frying pan, I wasn't going to get him to budge. OK, I probably wouldn't get him to budge even *with* the frying pan, but it sure would have made me feel better.

So I left, and I haven't seen him since, though I know he is there in the background, keeping an eye on me. He'd step in if I really needed him. So far I haven't. I guess it gives me some comfort to know he's there, just in case I needed protecting.

Stupid man. I really hate that his sense of honor, one of the things I truly admire about him, is the one thing that is keeping us apart. How can I argue with that? How can I hate him for that? Even though hating him would be so much easier than the pain that is currently ripping my heart to shreds.

Chapter One

Majicks and Potions. Eddie here." Eddie Mulligan runs an occult shop in Portland and has helped me out on more than one occasion.

"Hi, Eddie, it's Morgan. I need your help."

"Morgan!" His voice boomed cheerfully through my earpiece. "So good to hear from you. What do you need? Summoning potion? Banishing spell? Three-pronged crossbow arrows?"

"Three-pronged crossbow arrows? You've got those?"

"Of course!" His chuckle warmed my heart. Eddie has a way of making a person feel good, even when the proverbial shit is hitting the fan. Which it certainly was at the moment. "Shall I set some aside for you?"

"Now that you mention it, sure. But that's not what I called about. Do you know how to kill a keres?" The shit might have hit the fan with Jack, but there were still vampires to stake and demons to slay. No rest for the wicked.

I've been hunting vampires for the past three years—ever since one of them tried to put me in the ground permanently. Fortunately, he failed. I was resuscitated, but the attack left me with abilities far beyond that of normal humans, and Kabita Jones, who would become my boss and best friend, recruited me to hunt the hunters. But a keres was a new one for me.

The past week had been difficult, to say the least. Anger warred with frustration warred with pain. There is nothing quite like the hurt of thinking you have everything you ever wanted, needed, only to have it snatched away.

"A death spirit? Good lords above. Are you sure it's a keres?"

"That's what Trevor says," I assured him. Trevor, our lovely "handler," as he likes to call himself, is a royal pain in the ass if I ever met one, but when it comes to his requests, we don't have a choice. That is the deal. The government pays us big bucks; we do what they want. Mostly.

"There's a keres loose in the neighborhood," I continued. Kereses are death spirits—always female, incredibly rare, and incredibly difficult to kill. It usually takes a witch.

"No kidding? Isn't that more up Kabita's alley?"

I shrugged, even though I knew Eddie couldn't see me. "She's got stuff going on." The truth was, Kabita knew I needed to keep busy, so she'd been sending almost all the assignments my way. I guess she figured killing things would help keep my mind off Jack.

"Well then"—I heard Eddie clear his throat, his tone becoming serious—"you've got a problem. You can't *kill* a keres. A keres is a spirit, and spirits, as you know, are noncorporeal by their very essence. They turn corporeal only when they are about to feed."

"So, if I can't kill it, what do I do?"

"Banish it, of course." His voice had returned to its natural state of jubilance. I swear, Eddie couldn't be solemn for more than five minutes if his life depended on it. "It's really very simple. First, you need to call the darkness."

Oh, shit.

I really try to avoid using the darkness. It has a way of taking over and doing things I don't want it to do. Unfortunately, if I wanted to banish the death spirit, it sounded like I didn't have much of a choice.

The darkness had shown up in my life a couple months ago. About the same time I met Jack and got tangled up in the stupid

Heart of Atlantis business. I don't really know what the darkness is or where it came from or why I'm so lucky to have it, but it's there inside me. Lurking.

Oh, it has its good points. Like making me even stronger than my usual extrahuman strength. Faster. More ruthless. But it likes killing a whole lot more than I do, and sometimes…Let's just say the more I use it, the more it feels like it's trying to take over.

Gods only know what would happen if it did.

I rummaged around in the trunk of my Mustang sorting through my hunter paraphernalia. Among the assorted blades, stakes, crossbows, and experimental weaponry I use on vampires was a small jar of rock salt I keep for demonic emergencies. Not enough for a keres, that's for sure.

After stocking up on salt, I drove to the parking lot near the top of Rocky Butte, winding my way along the narrow road lined with expensive houses. No matter which side of the butte you're on, the view of Portland is amazing. In the distance, Mount Hood's perpetual snowcap gleamed a pale pink in the sunset.

I hiked up the short distance from the parking lot to the lookout at the top of the butte. It was pretty much the highest natural area in the eastern side of the city. Or at least the one with the best view. At some point, the top had been leveled flat, graveled, and ringed by a low stone wall. It was a popular spot for stargazing, but it was nearly dinnertime, so I had the place to myself, which was good. The last thing I needed was an audience.

I took a deep breath and closed my eyes. I focused deep down to that place inside where the darkness lives. A few months ago, I didn't even know it was there, but now it seems I no longer need to channel the darkness outside. The darkness *inside* writhes and seethes and is a living thing trapped within me, waiting to get out.

Sometimes it gets out on its own.

Now it was time to let it loose deliberately.

3

The darkness stirred, and I felt fear grip my heart in a vise. This wasn't good. Fear only makes the darkness harder to control. I shoved the fear down as best I could and focused on the thing living inside me.

I visualized holding on to the darkness like one might hold a dog on a leash. Then, holding fast to the end of the leash, I let the dog run.

The darkness heaved its way out of me with a shriek of relief, snapping my head back and nearly knocking me off my feet. It rushed through me, the pressure building until I wanted to scream. That was when I heard it: the hunting cry of the keres.

Eddie was right. The keres wasn't just attracted to death; it was attracted to darkness. It could feed on one as well as the other. And my darkness carries one hell of a wallop.

My eyes popped open, but it was like looking up through a dark, swirling well. The darkness was a vortex of rage and hunger that nearly consumed me. I could see the keres wheeling in the sky above me, black wings stretched against the dying rays of the sun. It screeched at me, as though hungry for the darkness that lives inside me.

The darkness screamed back.

The keres swooped down, bone-white fangs dripping with venom, eyes bloodred in a skull-like face. I shuddered. Fear mixed with exhilaration streaked through me as the darkness boiled and raged, reaching for its prey.

Before the darkness could take over, I shoved it down. It reared and snapped, but I wasn't about to allow it to control me, so I shoved harder. It resisted every inch of the way as I pushed against it with my mind. I was almost sure this would be the time it didn't go, but finally, I managed to thrust it down into that deep place within me where the darkness lives and slam the lid. I'd contained it. For now.

The keres swooped in, claws extended. I'd been distracted, and she was faster than I'd imagined. With a bloodcurdling scream, she swiped at me. I managed to turn and miss getting my face torn off, but one claw raked my back, leaving a huge gash in both my jacket and the flesh underneath.

For just a moment, I felt nothing and thought I'd escaped. Then the searing pain hit, setting my back on fire and nearly dropping me to my knees. I stumbled, narrowly avoiding another rake of the beast's claws.

I knew my weapons wouldn't do the keres any permanent harm, but I needed to fend her off long enough to do what needed to be done. I slid my dagger out of its sheath on my thigh. The blade glinted in the fading light as the keres dove for me again. This time I lashed out with the blade, separating a claw from her body.

Her scream was one of pain and rage as she reeled away. The claw lay twitching in the gravel like some macabre windup toy before it fizzled away into so much smoke. The keres wheeled in the sky before diving in for the kill. Determined bitch.

I reached into my pocket and came out with a handful of salt. Not that stupid table salt, either, but nice, big chunks of rock salt. I tossed it straight into her face.

She shrieked as the salt sizzled against her skin, and went tumbling ass over teakettle across the top of Rocky Butte, sending gravel spraying everywhere. I pulled out another handful of salt, and as I threw it over her, I yelled, "*Thuraze* keres, *ouk eni Anthesteria!*"

Which is apparently something along the lines of "Keres, I banish you!" in Greek, the original language of banishing spells for these demons. Granted it sounds a lot cooler in Greek.

The ground under the keres cracked open, and with a final angry shriek, she disappeared into the earth. Thank goodness Kabita had taught me that spell.

The darkness heaved up, making one last effort to escape. Panic warred with determination as I mentally grabbed its leash, willing it back down.

It didn't respond.

The darkness snapped and snarled, lunging against the metaphorical leash, while I hung on by not much more than sheer desperation. I couldn't let it out. There was no telling what it would do, but I knew it wouldn't be good.

Suddenly, it wheeled on me with a frightening snarl. For a moment, I thought it was going to swallow me up and spit me out. I can't even begin to explain the terror. So I did the one thing I could think of to do: I snarled back.

It hesitated, almost as if it were confused. That moment of hesitation gave me just enough time to slam the metaphorical lid down on it.

I wondered if someday I wouldn't be able to close that lid, but I shoved that thought aside. I had more important things to do than worry about someday.

I pulled out my phone and hit speed dial before sinking down onto the gravel. With the darkness gone, I could feel every ache and bruise. Shit, I was tired.

"Yeah." Kabita was her usual brusque self.

"It's finished."

She was silent a moment. "Good. Now, get back here. We have some things to discuss."

"Yes, ma'am." My voice was ever so slightly snarky.

I was splattered with demon goo and streaked with blood, and as I headed down the hill to the car, my ribs protested rather emphatically. The darkness had healed any cracks, but they were still plenty sore.

Back on terra firma, I turned the car toward the office. I probably should have cleaned up first, but Kabita had sounded like sooner would be a lot better than later. She'd just have to deal with the goo.

∽

"You're dripping blood on my carpet. Again."

"Well, at least this time it's black. That's a change," I said, pulling my shirt out away from my body and eyeballing the damage. Demon blood is often black or green. No idea why.

Kabita glared at me before tossing me a box of wet wipes. "Yes." Her voice was dry as dust. "That's such an improvement."

I shrugged and threw her a cheeky grin. "I do my best."

"The hunt went OK?" she asked.

"It was…interesting. Never hunted a keres before. Remind me to thank Agent Daly," I said.

"If you can spare a minute for us peasants, I've got another job for you." Kabita has been making cracks like that ever since I told her about the royal bloodline thing. Every time she does, it makes me think of Jack.

"I might be able to work something out," I said with an airy wave of my hand.

"I need you to take over for a couple days. Meet with clients. Deal with Daly."

I rolled my eyes. "Fun. My favorite person. What's going on?"

Kabita shook her head. "I have some things I need to take care of."

I eyed her across the desk. Fine lines between her eyes told me there was something wrong. Something she was trying to avoid talking about. "Tell me."

She sighed. "My cousin was murdered two days ago."

"Shit, Kabita, I'm sorry."

She shrugged. "These things happen sometimes. She knew the risks. I haven't seen her in several years, but we were close as children." It sounded cold, but I knew better. Kabita keeps her pain to herself. It's just her way.

I frowned. "The risks? Was she into drugs or something?"

She gave me the Look. "Don't be daft, Morgan. She was MI8."

Well, slap me with a wet noodle. MI8 is the British intelligence agency responsible for handling paranormal activity, mythical creatures, and things that go bump in the night. MI8 had "officially" ceased operations after World War II, but they continued their work in secret, though they didn't have the power they once did. They were the ones who locked my ass up back in the day to see if I would turn after my attack.

Something clicked together in my mind. A little piece of the puzzle I'd wondered about from time to time. It finally made sense how Kabita was able to get me out of MI8 custody so easily. She'd had a little inside help.

"Double shit. Vamp? Demon?" MI8 agents don't get murdered by normal people. Mostly because normal people don't even know MI8 exists.

"I don't know, but Dex asked me to come. I leave in a couple hours." Her face turned hard and cold, which was sort of spooky. She's always a little on the serious side, but this was something new. Something violent. It was not a side of her I'd ever seen before. "I'm going to kill the son of a bitch who hurt my family." Oh, yeah, this was serious. Kabita rarely swears.

"Fine. Sounds like a plan. I'm going with you. Give me time to shower and pack. You are not doing this thing alone."

Her smile was tight, but there was a flash of relief in her eyes. "Thanks."

I knew she'd never ask. But I also knew she'd need me. Not as a hunter, but as her friend. "That's what friends are for."

"I know what this might cost you."

She meant going back. Returning to London where I'd died— or not-died. But she was wrong. I love London. I am drawn to it.

Plus, the vampire who had killed me was still out there. He'd haunted my nightmares for three years. And while I'd never truly entertained the thought, somewhere in the back of my mind was the need to avenge myself. It was time for a little payback, not just for Kabita's cousin, but for me.

"You're wrong, Kabita." I stood up and headed out of the office. At the door, I turned back. "It won't cost me a thing. I plan on collecting on an old debt." I could feel the smile stretching across my face. It wasn't a happy smile.

For the first time, Kabita looked just a little bit scared. I wasn't sure whether she was scared of me or for me. Then she nodded. "Two hours."

Chapter Two

I sank into the roomy leather seat with a sigh of relief. That's one thing about having your own hunter agency—never having to fly coach again. Thanks to Uncle Sam's very generous compensation package for our work ridding society of supernatural menaces, Kabita is able to hire a private jet anytime a case takes us away from Portland. Makes life a lot easier. Hard to explain to the TSA why you need to check a suitcase full of weaponry.

I made sure my portable weapons locker was locked and stowed safely under my seat. The UK has strict weapons laws. Fortunately, they are also used to hunters, and Kabita's brother, Dex, had already cleared us through customs. Pays to know people in high places.

I wiggled a little, so the leather squeaked under my butt. Yeah, this was living. I wondered if they'd serve lobster. Not that I like lobster. In fact, I loathe seafood, but it's the thought that counts.

"Don't worry, there's no lobster." Kabita dropped into the seat next to me. "It's salmon."

I must have turned pale because she burst out laughing. Of all the fish in all the world, salmon is the rankest. She chuckled. "I ordered a vegetarian meal for you."

"I will love you forever," I said, rather more fervently than strictly necessary.

She shook her head as she settled back into the plush seat and pulled out a stack of files. It was clear she had no intention of discussing the situation with her family or her cousin's death, and although my mind burned with questions, I knew there was no way to budge her. I'd find out the answers soon enough.

I'd always thought it a bit strange that Kabita seemed much closer to her cousin Inigo, who worked with us in Portland, than she was to her own brothers. But I'd always supposed that was because they still lived in the UK along with her father.

What I know about the rest of Kabita's family could fill a thimble. She doesn't like talking about them. All I know is that while her mother's family came from India, her father is some sort of English muckety-muck. His family has a lot of power and influence in the British government, especially with agencies like MI8, the supposedly disbanded agency for the study of the paranormal and supernatural. How he ended up married to an Indian woman from a tiny village in Malaysia is most likely an interesting tale, though I've never heard it. In any case, he did, and Kabita and her brothers were all raised in the same village in Malaysia until they were old enough to attend university. Then they'd all hit the UK. And stayed.

I know her dad never left the UK other than for brief visits to his wife and kids in Malaysia while the kids were growing up. And now I know she has a cousin in MI8—or rather, who had formerly been with MI8 and now lies dead in the morgue somewhere. And that is all I know about the family of Kabita Jones, my best friend and boss.

Maybe it's odd that I've never pressed her about her family, but I've always been of the opinion that, for the most part, people will share their personal stuff when they're good and ready.

I decided all work and no play made for a very dull life, indeed, so I snagged a book out of my carry-on and settled in. I tried to read, but my brain wouldn't settle down and focus. I just kept replaying my last visit with Jack over and over in my mind.

Being with him had been amazing. I'd been so sure I was finally on the verge of happily ever after. Or as close to happily ever after as anyone can come in this life. Then everything had gone to hell in a handbasket.

One minute we'd been getting our sexy on, and then the next he was bowing and scraping like I was some gods-damned queen of the freaking Nile or something. All because I touched that amulet. Or rather, because I'd touched it and it decided to turn into a blue-light special.

We'd been so close to something real. My throat got tight just thinking about it, and I could feel the hot tears threatening to spill over. I shook my head and swallowed them back. No way was I breaking down.

I sighed. Jack was going to be seriously pissed when he figured out I'd flown to London without him. But I wouldn't be a very good hunter if I couldn't slip my own bodyguard now and then.

Heathrow was just as mental as I remembered it. In some ways, it is actually rather beautiful, all gleaming marble and shiny steel, with loads and loads of highly polished glass. In other ways, it is a total nightmare—people running everywhere, noise and light and complete craziness. It is a great place to people watch, though, and I smiled as reunited friends and relatives embraced each other with unbridled enthusiasm.

"Come on." Kabita motioned toward the huge bank of elevators just outside the arrival doors. "Dex is meeting us outside Departures."

That meant we had to go down one floor and out the sky bridge. I hoped Kabita's brother wasn't late. I was exhausted and felt like I hadn't bathed in a year. A shower was definitely in order.

As we headed toward the lifts, a young woman coming the other way brushed past us. I wouldn't have paid her any attention except that when she saw Kabita, she got the oddest look on her face—a strange mix of surprise, anger, and glee. Then she was gone.

"Um, Kabita, did you see that girl?"

She turned, and one silky black brow went up. "What girl?"

"The one who just passed us." I jerked my head in the direction she'd disappeared.

She shook her head and kept walking. "Wasn't paying that much attention. Why?"

I shrugged. "I don't know. She acted like maybe she knew you or recognized you or something. It was weird."

"What did she look like?" She propped herself against the wall of the elevator and waited for it to descend to the ground floor. The elevators in Terminal 5 were all automated and ran in a particular cycle. I'd seen more than one tourist standing around looking absolutely baffled trying to figure out where the call button is.

"Really short platinum-blonde hair. Kind of spiky. Brown eyes. About my height. Looked like she had a tattoo on her arm, but I didn't catch what it was." She also moved just like a hunter, but I didn't mention that. London, after all, is full of hunters. In a city of more than eight million people, there is plenty of work for them. I ought to know.

Kabita shook her head, frowning. "Doesn't ring any bells. It's possible I did a job or something for her in the past, I guess."

I shook my head. "Too young. She looked like she was barely out of her teens."

"Maybe I've just got one of those faces." Her voice was dry.

I burst out laughing. "Sure. That must be it." There may be some people who have bland, ordinary looks, people who blend into the crowd, but Kabita Jones isn't one of those people. With her cloud of waist-length jet-black hair and cinnamon skin, she stands out anywhere, even in a multicultural city like London.

Kabita's brother had gotten a spot right near the sky bridge. Brownie points to him. At least we didn't have to trudge all over creation just to find the car.

Dexter Jones looks nothing like his sister. Granted, he has the same black hair and cinnamon skin, but the similarities end there.

While Kabita is actually a couple inches shorter than my own five foot five, Dex towers over both of us at a good six foot two. Also, while Kabita has her mother's more exotic Indian features, Dex's are pure Anglo, right down to his gray eyes and slightly Romanesque nose. Dex must take after their father. And while Kabita's accent still holds the music of her Malaysian childhood, despite twenty years living in England and another three in the United States, Dex's accent is pure London—the posh side of London.

Dex helped us load our suitcases into the trunk of his car. "Thanks for coming."

Kabita nodded. "Of course."

Once we were settled in the car with Dex in the driver's seat, Kabita said, "Tell me."

Dex was quiet as he steered the car out into traffic. When he finally spoke, his voice was tight. "I think it's best if you wait to talk to Dad."

Personally, I would have pushed him for more info, and I expected Kabita to do the same. But she knows her brother better than I do.

She just sighed. "When does he want to meet?"

"Tonight. Eight o'clock. The Cinnamon Club." He glanced at her. "Missed you, K."

She smiled and reached over to squeeze his arm.

Man of few words, I guess. But I was excited about the meeting place. The Cinnamon Club is quite possibly the poshest Indian restaurant in the whole of London. The food is supposed to be beyond amazing. When I lived in London, I'd never been able to afford a place like that.

"Fine," Kabita said. "I'll wait. But you know I don't like this."

It was an odd thing to say, but Dex just shrugged.

I wondered about her relationship with her family. My mother and grandmother drive me nuts pretty much on a daily basis, but I've always wondered what it would be like if my dad were still alive. Maybe we'd be a real family then. Kabita seems unusually distant with hers. Except maybe Dex. There is genuine warmth there, if a little strained.

Not my business. I stared out the window, enjoying the sights of the city that had once been my home. I felt a sharp stab of nostalgia.

"Got a date or something?" Kabita asked in a low voice.

"What?"

"You keep checking your phone."

I shook my head. "Just wondering if I have time before dinner."

"For what?"

I shrugged. "A hunt."

She gave me a look that clearly said she knew what I meant. A hunt for the vamp who killed me three years ago. "You don't." Her tone was firm as we slid out of the car.

"I'll pick you up at fifteen to eight," Dex said.

Kabita didn't answer, but he obviously took her silence as consent. I caught his eye in the rearview mirror, and the smile he gave me was a little sad around the edges.

I wondered whether the sadness was because of the death of their cousin or the strain in the relationship with his sister. Maybe it was a little of both. I smiled back. It was all I had to give.

Chapter Three

The Cinnamon Club stands on Great Smith Street in Westminster. It is a gorgeous redbrick building that once housed the old Westminster Library, back when libraries were all mellow wood and dim lamps instead of bright beacons of glass and steel.

Dex pulled the car up to the curb and turned off the engine. "Ready?" he asked Kabita. She nodded, every line of her body screaming the exact opposite.

Curiouser and curiouser.

He escorted us inside the restaurant. It was even more beautiful than the outside. Crystal and silver sparkled in the candlelight while old wood gleamed gently, lending the place an atmosphere of sophisticated elegance.

I felt only slightly out of place. I don't really do elegant dining. I usually end up feeling like a bull in a china shop. Fortunately, I am also really good at hiding my insecurities.

The air was redolent with the scent of Indian cooking spices: cinnamon, cardamom, turmeric, chilies, and curry leaves. Gods, I'd missed this. The little hole-in-the-wall Indian dive Kabita and I frequent back in Portland is good, but it has nothing on the kind of Indian you can find in the restaurants of London.

Dex led us to a secluded table off to one side. Its sole occupant stood to greet us.

He was tall, nearly as tall as Dex. His charcoal suit was beautifully cut and perfectly tailored to show off a lean physique, and his ice-gray eyes seemed to miss nothing. Despite his silver hair and pale skin, there was no doubt at all that Dex was his son. Kabita, on the other hand, looked nothing like her father.

"Dad." Kabita's voice, always calm and cool, held zero emotion. Her face was devoid of expression. "This is my friend Morgan Bailey."

Not "my colleague." Not "my fellow hunter." "My friend." Interesting.

Apparently, her dad thought so too. His perfectly groomed left eyebrow went up. Oh, yeah, *now* I know where Kabita got it.

"Morgan Bailey. At last we meet. I've heard much about you from my friends at the SRA. As I'm sure you must know, I'm Alister Jones. Welcome back to London." His handshake was firm, voice the utterly polished and carefully modulated tone of the upper-class English gentleman.

I wondered who at the Supernatural Regulatory Agency had been talking about me, but I wasn't going to ask. Instead, I smiled and resisted the urge to tell him that while he may have heard about me, I'd heard nothing about him. Didn't think Kabita would appreciate my getting all snarky with her dad.

"Thank you. It's good to be back." I meant it. Portland might be my home and the city of my birth, but London is still in my blood. I don't think it will ever come out.

"Where are Adler and Adam?" Kabita's voice was still very nearly expressionless as she settled into her chair. The cold front between her and her dad was nearly palpable. What was with this family? Seriously, they were taking the whole British stiff-upper-lip thing way too far.

I took my own seat, assisted by Dex. Kabita was starting to worry me. Her manner wasn't the only thing that had changed since we'd arrived in London. She'd altered her appearance as well. For dinner, she'd dressed in a sleek navy-blue dress and put her hair up in an elegant bun thing like a ballerina. Every little wisp of hair was perfectly in place. Worst of all, she was wearing pearls like freaking Donna Reed. Creepy.

She must have noticed me gawking at her, as she suddenly started toying with the creamy pearl bracelet on her left wrist—a sure sign she felt uncomfortable.

"The twins are on assignment." Alister Jones's voice was as cool as his daughter's. "They don't know about your cousin yet." Something moved behind his eyes, something hard and very, very angry. Contrary to outward appearances, he was pissed as hell. I wasn't sure whether his anger was due to his niece's death or the fact that his sons weren't there to share in the family tragedy. Possibly, it was something else altogether. All I knew was it made me very uncomfortable and set off a whole bunch of alarm bells in my head.

I probably shouldn't butt into family business, but this was no ordinary family, and I was no ordinary friend.

I looked Alister Jones straight in the eye and said, "What was her name?"

"Julia. Her name was Julia."

"Julia Jones?"

"No. She was my sister's child. It was Julia Reynolds." He took out his wallet and pulled a photograph from it. He held on to it for a moment, his face void of expression, before handing it to me.

Julia Reynolds had been beautiful, no doubt about that. Golden ringlets surrounded a heart-shaped face, framing the biggest blue eyes I'd ever seen and pouty pink lips that would make Angelina Jolie pea green with envy. Her smile held no hint that she spent her life dealing with monsters and the carnage they left behind.

I wondered how she could do her job and still look so damn sunny. I guess when the monsters actually look like monsters, it's easier to deal with than the human beings who do monstrous things. I should know—I live my life among the monsters. I understand them.

Sometimes I think I understand them just a little too well.

I shoved that thought aside very quickly. I didn't have time to think about the weirdness that has become my life or the darkness that now lurks constantly just beyond my sight. Waiting. Always waiting.

Kabita shook her head slightly as though to clear her thoughts. "How did she die?"

Alister motioned her to wait as a bevy of waiters approached the table loaded down with steaming platters and bowls. The smell wafting off those dishes was so delectable it set my stomach rumbling.

"I took the liberty of ordering for us all. I thought we'd share." For just a moment, Alister's smile was genuine and warm. It reminded me of Kabita's. Perhaps she is her father's daughter, after all.

Kabita and Dex murmured their approval, while I tried hard not to salivate. I helped myself to a piece of naan lightly brushed with butter. Perfect.

As we dug in, Alister told us about the death of Julia Reynolds.

"Like most of our family, Julia started working for MI8 as soon as she left university," Alister began. His voice was calm, detached, as though he were talking about a stranger instead of his own niece. I guess we all deal with grief in different ways.

I gave Kabita a look out of the corner of my eye, but her expression remained bland. I knew for a fact that Kabita had never worked for MI8. Interesting.

"Julia wasn't a field agent. Her specialty was research, and she was particularly good at it. She had a knack for uncovering the truth. More than one life was saved over the years because of her instincts and her unwavering dedication to doing what she believed was right." There was an edge to his voice at that. One that told me he hadn't quite approved of Julia's dedication to truth. I filed it away for future reference.

"Unwavering dedication to the truth is a good way to get yourself killed," I pointed out. "Truth is usually hidden for a reason." *Though not always a good one.* I kept that thought to myself. I wanted to play along with Alister a little. See if I could peek beneath the icy veneer of the man.

Alister nodded in agreement. "That was Julia's downfall. She didn't know when to back down and turn her research over to someone more qualified for the dangerous work. The very focus that made her good at her job also made her tempting to kill. Obviously, someone finally gave in to temptation."

Tempting to kill? Now, that was an interesting phrase.

Kabita scowled slightly but didn't openly disagree with Alister. I had the feeling she'd admired Julia's tenacity far more than her father did. I was all for girls kicking ass but could see his point. As a researcher, Julia no doubt hadn't been trained the way Kabita and I had. She hadn't had the skills to protect herself.

There is a fine line between determination and stupidity. From the sounds of things, Julia had stepped over that line one too many times, and now she was dead. Didn't make it right, just made it a fact.

"What was she working on?" Kabita asked.

"Nothing official," Alister said. "But for the past year, she'd been pursuing her own project. She didn't say much about it." He appeared to brush it off as unimportant.

Dex spoke up. "I got the impression it was something big. I know she was spending a lot of time in the oldest sections of the MI8 archives. I also know she'd been in contact with several police departments around the world regarding some of their cases."

That caught my attention. "Cases involving what?"

Dex shook his head. "No idea. Julia had a lot of autonomy, and she wasn't interested in sharing. We found nothing on her work computers, and her personal laptop is missing."

"So, whatever it was she was working on, you think she was killed because of it?" I asked. It made sense.

"It is likely, yes," Alister said. There was something about his expression, a sort of shifty look in his eyes, that didn't sit well with me. I had the feeling he knew more than he was telling. "She could have been killed either because of something she found or something she was about to find."

"How was she killed?"

Alister shook his head and took a deep draft of wine. You aren't supposed to gulp wine like that, and Alister struck me as the kind of guy with proper table manners. He was either a lot more upset about his niece's death than he was letting on or there was something else bothering him. It was Dex who finally told me.

"When she didn't show up for work, her supervisor rang me. I popped over to her flat and found her…" His voice went a little hoarse, and he had to cough to clear it. "I won't show you the photos here, but she was ripped open, neck to groin. Three slashes. Her chest cavity looked as though someone had torn her rib cage apart like a pea pod." His hand shook a little as he raised his water glass.

My mouth went a little dry. "Was it one continuous movement? Or lots of smaller motions?"

"That's not important," Alister interrupted. "MI8 is investigating the matter. You're here for the funeral. Nothing more."

"Actually, *Father*," Kabita said the word like it was dirty, "we were invited by MI8 to assist in the investigation."

"I authorized no such invitation."

"I asked her," Dex said. His voice was firm. He might be Alister's subordinate, technically speaking, but it was obvious Dex had a whole lot of pull at MI8 all on his own.

The look on Alister's face could only be described as repressed fury. Still, he schooled it well, turning his expression to one of polite blandness. "Very well."

"The slashing movement?" I prompted Dex.

"One continuous."

A jolt of shock coursed through me.

I knew of only one creature strong enough to slash some-one from stem to stern and crack open a pair of ribs with a sin-gle slash. And yet what I suspected wasn't possible. Kabita was unusually silent, eating her way through her dinner almost like she was on autopilot, so I kept up with the questions. "Were any of her organs missing?"

Dex looked a little pale. "Yeah. Her heart."

I frowned at that. There should have been more missing than just the heart. A lot more. "Was anything left behind?"

Dex nodded as he took something from his pocket and placed it on the table. It was about the size and diameter of an oyster, but flat and paper thin. In the dim light of the restaurant, it shimmered blue and green and gold with just a hint of pink. Like abalone shell, but with more vibrant colors.

I picked it up and turned it over in my hands, running my fin-gers along the subtle ridges. I expected it to be cool to the touch, but it was strangely warm. My hands tingled slightly, as though I'd received a slight electric shock, except it wasn't the type of mate-rial to hold static electricity. Odd.

I tried to snap it between my fingers, but it didn't give even a fraction, despite its delicate appearance. I picked up one of the steak knives and tried to cut the disc, but the blade didn't even scratch the surface.

Holy crikey heck. There was no way what I was thinking could be true. It wasn't possible. They were extinct. They had been for aeons. Even their bones had turned to dust long ago. Yet there it was in my hands. Proof.

It was no shell. A shell would have broken into pieces. It defi-nitely would have scratched under the blade, probably shattered. This was something else entirely. But the pieces still didn't fit. Not quite.

"Are you sure only her heart was missing?"

Dex and Alister both nodded.

"The rest of her...insides were scooped out and scattered around the room, but only the heart was missing." Dex's voice was grim. I couldn't blame him. Just the thought was enough to turn my stomach.

But that fit. Or at least the part about the organs being scooped out did.

I gave Kabita a look and saw she was frowning too. The same thought was running through both our minds, and we both were struggling because it didn't make sense, and yet it was the only thing that did. What I didn't understand was how both Alister and Dex had missed it.

"What is it?" Alister leaned forward almost eagerly. "You know something. What is it?"

"I suspect something," I admitted. "But I can't be sure. Some of the facts don't add up."

He leaned forward in his chair, food and wine completely forgotten. "Tell me."

"The slashes, the opened rib cage, the missing heart, the scattered entrails, even this scale." I held it up. Because that's what it was. A scale. Armor plating. Natural armor plating for something really, really big. "They could only mean one thing. It all fits. The problem is, it shouldn't. It goes against everything science and history has taught us." Then again, so do sunwalkers.

"What fits? What killed my niece?" He was angry now. Impatient. But there was an eagerness there too. Definitely odd.

If I was wrong about this, I would create some temporary chaos. Piss some people off. But if I was right? Then I could start a war. I sighed. This was not a good time to be right.

"I could be wrong, but from the looks of things, Julia was killed by something that's not even supposed to exist anymore."

"What?" he practically snarled at me.

I sighed and ran a hand through my hair. This was not going to go down well. "It looks like Julia was killed by a dragon."

Chapter Four

Alister and Dex stared at me as though I'd suddenly grown a second head. I got that. It isn't every day someone blames a murder on a dragon. Especially since dragons had supposedly died out centuries ago.

"That's ridiculous," Alister scoffed. "It might look like a dragon scale, but there is no way…They're extinct."

"Did you just say dragon?" Dex repeated.

"Yeah, I did." I slammed the scale down hard on the edge of the table. It gave a dull thunk but was otherwise unaffected. "This isn't metal or stone. If this were just about anything else, it would have broken. It doesn't scratch, either. I'll bet if we try to melt it, we'll find it's resistant to fire. And look"—I tilted it toward the light—"it shimmers, changes color like abalone." I'd read up a bit on dragons in my spare time. It's one of those things that has always fascinated me, especially when I found out they were real. Or had been. Their scales fit the bill perfectly.

"This is a dragon scale." Kabita sounded gobsmacked. I couldn't blame her. It was pretty cool.

"You're sure?" Alister's voice still had that strange edge of eagerness. It made me uncomfortable, though I couldn't put my finger on why. I can read vampires like a book, but my Spidey senses don't really work with humans.

"Yes, I believe so." I ran my thumb over the warm surface and felt a thrill run through me. My heart pumped a little faster. I was holding a real honest-to-gods dragon scale. It was like finding the

Holy Grail or something. "Interesting, though, since according to what I've read, dragons are supposed to be extinct."

Alister didn't comment, and Kabita narrowed her eyes at him. "The hunter records state that dragons were hunted to extinction nearly four hundred years ago. You have anything to add to that? *Dad?*" Her voice dripped with sarcasm. Kabita is really good at sarcasm.

Alister gave her a look before calmly returning to his curry. "Not here, Kabita." It was clear from his reaction that he knew far more about the dragon issue than he was letting on.

I glanced around at the other diners. They looked harmless enough in their Savile Row suits and Manolo Blahnik heels. Plus, we were sitting pretty far away from anyone else. He was right, though. Too many eyes and ears. Very cloak and dagger, but anyone could be hiding in the crowd.

Even if the restaurant were spy-free, there were still plenty of innocent, ordinary citizens who'd be none too thrilled to hear there were dragons on the loose. *If* there were dragons on the loose. The last thing we needed was full-blown panic running though the streets of London.

I turned the scale over in my hands again, for once completely distracted from my dinner. What I held was something akin to a scroll from the lost Library of Alexandria. If I weren't actually holding the thing in my hands, gliding my fingertips over its smooth surface, I would have never believed it was real.

I glanced back up at Alister, then over at Dex. "You want to find out who killed Julia? We need some answers."

Dex gave his father a determined look. "She's right, Dad. They need to know more if they're going to figure out this thing."

I could tell Alister was still none too thrilled about having Kabita and me on the case, but he gave me a regal nod that was just a tad too theatrical. "Soon," he agreed. "Soon."

I glanced at Kabita. Her expression was stony as she focused on the plate in front of her. She didn't want to rock the boat? Fine. But this was a boat that needed to be rocked. I was starting to get tired of all the nonanswers. Kabita's dad or not, if he didn't start cluing us in soon, I was going to get bitchy.

It wasn't the British way to get all up in someone's face, but I'd been away from London too long, and this was too important to play the game of being civil. Because if I was right about the dragon thing, a lot of lives were in danger.

"By soon, I mean today," I said. "You don't want to talk here? Fine, I get that. It's clear you don't want us involved in this investigation, but you're wrong. Trust me, you do. We're damn good at what we do, so if you want this thing solved, you'd better get us somewhere you *can* talk. Now."

I didn't know who was more surprised—Kabita, because someone finally talked back to her dad, or Alister himself, because someone had the cojones to call his bullshit.

"What'll it be, Alister?" I let the dragon scale catch the light, reminding him of what was at stake.

I'm not sure what he saw in my eyes, but whatever it was must have convinced him that I was 100 percent serious. And I was. I'd had my fill of secrets and lies. I wanted the truth, and Alister Jones could either give it to me or he could shove off.

"Fine." His voice was rife with irritation. "Dex, go get the car."

I smiled as I slipped the scale into my purse. No way was I handing it back to Alister Jones. I didn't trust the man. Not by half. Something about him didn't add up.

Dex, looking somewhat bemused, tossed his napkin on the table and headed for the front door, while Alister glanced at the headwaiter. Within minutes, the bill had been paid and we were on our way out the door. I guess that's the kind of service you get when you dine Michelin.

Dex hurried to open the back door for Alister like he was Little Lord Fauntleroy while Kabita hopped into the front. Apparently, being a guest meant I got the honor of riding in the back with the big man. I started to speak, but he held up his hand. "Not here. One never knows who is listening. Dex, head for the bridge."

I could deal with that. I settled back into the plush leather seats, determined to enjoy the ride as we drove past tall buildings of mellow stone, built when steam power had been no more than a dream. We turned left on Embankment and drove along the wide street with the river on our right. We passed Cleopatra's Needle. The Ancient Egyptian obelisk, which had once stood watch over the Nile, now guards the River Thames.

It wasn't a long ride. Fifteen minutes later, Dex was pulling into Saint Katherine's Dock, and Alister was ushering us from the car. I've always enjoyed Saint Katherine's Dock. Best view of the Tower Bridge in London. Tourists usually think it is the London Bridge because it is the fanciest one, but it was named after the London Tower, which lurks at the base of the bridge.

"We're all right here?" I asked Dex.

He nodded. "Yes. We should be fine." He turned to Alister. "Tell them."

Alister sighed. "I suppose I should tell you about the dragons first."

"Yeah, that would be a good place to start." I leaned my elbows against the cold metal railing and let my gaze wander out across the Thames. I still didn't entirely trust the man, but I wanted to hear what he had to say.

"Very well, I shall go back to the beginning." He leaned next to me while Kabita and Dex sat on a bench next to us, eyes on their father.

I nodded. "Also a good place to start. Where's the beginning?"

"About seventeen hundred years ago."

"So, not a short story, then?" I let a thread of amusement color my voice.

"Not really, no." Alister smiled, but there was an edge of tension to it. I was beginning to realize that Alister is not a very comfortable man. "Let me try to hit the important bits."

He was quiet for a moment, staring out over the water, gathering his thoughts. "About two thousand years ago, this country was being ravaged by dragons. Most of the world, in fact, lived in fear of the creatures. It had been going on for millennia. Between the dragons' monstrous appetites for flesh, both human and animal, and their vast intellect, our somewhat primitive ancestors didn't stand a chance."

Not really something one learned in history class, but the books I'd read had touched on it. There hadn't been a lot of detail, though, and certainly nothing to explain their extinction. "Something obviously changed," I prompted, "or we wouldn't be here."

He nodded, silver hair gleaming in the dim orange light from a nearby streetlamp. That was one thing it had taken me a while to get used to when I first moved to London. Streetlamps in the UK are dim orange instead of bright yellow or white. Energy saving or something. "Yes. Something did change. The first dragon hunter was born," Alister said.

I blinked. I like to read, and the histories of the hunters make for some interesting reading, but I'd never heard of a dragon hunter. I exchanged looks with Kabita. She shrugged. Clearly she'd never heard of them, either. I opened my mouth to say so, but Alister held up his hand.

"There were reasons dragon hunters were expunged from history. I'll explain later. First, let me tell the tale in my own way."

I nodded in agreement.

"The first dragon hunter was born to a poor family in Athens in the year AD three eleven. His name was Georgos."

No freaking way. "You mean Saint George? I thought he wasn't around until the Middle Ages."

Alister shrugged. "Every legend has its roots in reality. Even the legend of Saint George and the dragon, which was based on a real man born nearly eight hundred years earlier."

"So, George was real and he was a dragon hunter?" Weirder and weirder.

Alister gazed up at the bridge, but I wasn't sure he was seeing it. "Yes, he was real. Born at a time when it seemed the human race was doomed to extinction. To this day, we don't know where the dragons came from. It's possible they may have evolved here on earth, but how they existed for so long without annihilating everything…We just don't know. They were so incredibly destructive.

"In any case, when Georgos was a small boy, his village was razed by dragons, his entire family killed. The local monastery took him in, along with a few other boys who survived, but it wasn't long before they discovered he was different. Much different.

"One particular monk had been trained as a vampire hunter. He recognized the signs of another hunter, so he began to train Georgos. The boy was a quick study. By the time he was fourteen, he'd surpassed his teacher.

"One day, Georgos came running into the chapel while the monks were at prayers, screaming at everyone to hide in the cellars. The monastery was under attack by a dragon. Then he took up a sword and ran to the courtyard of the monastery. There, within the shadow of the chapel walls, he fought and killed his first dragon."

"Surely people had killed dragons before." I wasn't gullible enough to believe Saint George was the only person who'd ever killed a dragon prior to that day.

"True. Others had killed dragons before, but never a single man. Always it had taken whole villages or large numbers of heavily armed militia to take down one of the beasts. Never a man hardly more than a child armed with nothing but a sword. And there was something else." He hesitated, but I already knew.

"He could feel them, the dragons," I said. "He felt it coming; that's how he was able to warn the monks." Just like I could feel vampires. The thought made me shiver.

"Yes. That's what he told the abbot. Despite his bravery and the fact that he'd saved the entire monastery, he was cast out, along with his teacher. The monks claimed his gift was evil, from the devil. Ridiculous, of course, but from then on, the two of them wandered Europe together, killing dragons."

"You said he was the first dragon hunter," I pointed out. "There were others?" I glanced over at Kabita and Dex. From the look on Dex's face, I could tell he'd heard it before. Kabita looked as surprised as I felt.

"Yes, of course. Just as there are demon hunters and vampire hunters and so on today, back then there were also dragon hunters. Most hunters were ordinary men specially trained and well armed, but there were a few true dragon hunters, like Georgos, who were born with a little something extra. They were faster, stronger, than ordinary men. And they could sense the dragons long before they could see them. For the first time, people weren't sitting around waiting for the dragons to attack so they could defend themselves."

So the dragon hunters had the same kind of superpowers I do, only for dragons. That was actually pretty cool. "They took the war to the dragons," I guessed.

He nodded. "Yes. And within a few generations, they'd nearly wiped the dragons out."

I narrowed my eyes. "Nearly?"

"Georgos had a son, also a dragon hunter. He had a son and so on down the line. Every male in his line was born with the same ability to sense the dragons. Each was a formidable hunter, and each in his turn became leader of the dragon hunters.

"Eventually, the dragons learned to communicate with our kind, and sometime around AD five twenty-five, the dragon king approached the lead hunter under a flag of truce. By that time, the dragons were nearly extinct. If the slaughter continued, they would cease to exist. Like any creature, the dragons wanted to survive, to ensure their children would survive. So they made a pact with the dragon hunters. The dragons would stop killing, remove themselves to the most remote places of the earth, vanish from the world of humans. In return, the hunters agreed to stop hunting them and act simply as guardians."

"They agreed to guard the dragons? Were they insane?"

Alister shook his head. "It was a tactical move. By that time Dragons had recognized humans as intelligent and stopped using them as a food source, but many human lives had been lost in the wars, thanks to their bloodthirsty revenge. So many towns laid waste. The fighting had to stop before both sides were destroyed.

"The dragons, surprisingly, kept their word. They vanished. After centuries, the dragon hunters finally withdrew, no longer needed. It's been more than four hundred years, and no one has seen nor heard from a dragon in all that time. We'd assumed they had finally died off."

I thought for a moment. Things were beginning to click into place. "The records were altered to protect the dragons that remained."

"Yes. About a century later. By then it was felt that genocide would be…wrong." Again, there was something odd in his voice. I couldn't put my finger on it, but something felt off.

"Unusual for the time. What happened to the dragon hunters?"

"Most of them were assimilated into the other hunter groups," he said.

"And the others?" I prompted. I had a feeling there was more.

He stared out over the river for a moment, then heaved a sigh. "The ones who were like Georgos, the ones who were born to hunt the dragons, they didn't adjust quite as well."

"They went bonkers, didn't they?" I knew it deep down inside, where the part of me that senses the vamps lives. If I had no vamps to hunt, to kill, I'd probably end up mad as a hatter too. Fortunately for me, there seems to be a never-ending supply of the suckers.

"Yes." His voice was quiet, restrained, as if he felt the pain of men who'd died many hundreds of years ago. "Some of them made Jack the Ripper look like a joke. They had to be eliminated. The others, the ones who weren't quite as bad, were locked away so they couldn't hurt themselves or anyone else. Eventually, whatever it was that made them the way they were, it vanished from the gene pool. There hasn't been a dragon hunter born since the Crusades. The historical records were altered, deleting any reference to the dragon hunters. Only a single copy of the true record was kept, and only those at the highest levels could access that copy."

I shook my head. "More lies."

"It was necessary, Morgan. Not only to protect the dragons, but to avoid a panic over dragons, or worse, another witch hunt—this time against the dragon hunters."

I sighed and tipped my head back to catch a glimpse of the stars. I couldn't. The lights under the Tower Bridge were far too bright. That's the problem with living in a city.

Alister was right: things haven't changed much in the past few hundred years. People are still afraid of what they don't understand. And what they fear, they tend to destroy. What a frigging mess.

"I assume you've read the real records. That's how you know all this."

"Yes, of course. I am the head of MI8. It is my job to know such things. The dragons withdrew behind Hadrian's Wall and vanished."

"Hadrian's Wall. No kidding?"

"You don't think the Romans built that thing just to keep the Celts out, do you?" There was laughter in his voice.

I grinned back. "No, I suppose not. The dragons? You're sure no one's heard from them?" I asked. It seems incredible the huge beasts had just simply vanished.

"As I said, not since the last guardian was withdrawn from Hadrian's Wall more than three hundred years ago."

I lifted the scale to the dim light from the streetlamp, turning it back and forth, letting the warmth trickle down my skin. "Well, Alister, they're talking now."

Chapter Five

Alister sighed as he stepped back from the railing. "Right."

"Damn skippy."

A smile tugged at the corner of his mouth. "Nevertheless, it is not what I wanted to hear."

I shrugged. What else was there to say?

He turned toward the bench where Kabita had been studiously avoiding looking at him. "Will you see this through?" So now he wanted us to help. I sure wished he'd make up his mind.

Her voice held just a hint of frost. "Of course. Julia was my cousin. I won't let this stand."

Boy, I'd have hated to be the person responsible for Julia's death just then. Kabita sounded downright scary.

He nodded. "Very good. Well, ladies, I appreciate your time. If you don't mind, I have a few things to take care of tonight, so Dex will see you back to the hotel." So formal, I had to refrain from smirking.

"What about you, Dad? Are you sure I can't drop you somewhere?" I couldn't tell whether Dex was just being polite or if he was actually concerned about his father. The whole family dynamic was just plain odd. Alister was the oddest of all.

"Thank you, no. I fancy a walk."

Dex nodded and motioned us toward the parking lot. As we headed to the car, I cast a quick glance back. Alister stood at the rail, staring over the water. I didn't think I'd ever seen anyone so alone.

∽

"I think I'm going to head over to the old neighborhood."

Kabita paused in the midst of hanging up her jacket. "Do you think that's wise?" She carefully closed the wardrobe door as I leaned up against the doorjamb between our connecting hotel rooms.

We'd invited Dex to join us for a drink, but he'd politely refused. Probably for the best. Jet lag was starting to take its toll. Still, I knew I wouldn't sleep. Not yet.

"Probably not," I admitted. "But it's something I have to do." She didn't say anything, so I told her, "I dream about it sometimes."

She sighed as she sank down onto the edge of the bed. "I'm not surprised. That's not the sort of thing a person can forget."

No. It isn't. You generally don't forget the day you died. I changed the subject. "You hear from Inigo?" I'd been surprised he hadn't made the trip with us. Julia was his cousin too, but Kabita had said something about him hating funerals and someone needing to mind the shop anyway.

Kabita kicked off her shoes and left them where they fell. Funny. I am usually the messy one.

She shook her head. "It's still early back home, and you know how he is." She ran her fingers through her hair, and her hand shook just a little.

"You OK?" It was obvious that seeing her father again hadn't been an easy thing, though I'd no idea why. She and Dex had seemed OK, though. I was glad about that. For her sake.

She waved me off. "I'll be fine. I'd just like to be alone for a while. We'll talk tomorrow, all right?"

36

I nodded. "Yeah, OK." I turned and started to shut the door behind me, but her voice stopped me.

"You be careful out there."

"I'm always careful."

She rolled her eyes. "Yeah, sure you are."

I laughed. "Sarcastic witch."

Francois was on me the minute I entered the hotel lobby. The effervescent Frenchman was in charge of making sure the hotel guests were looked after, and I'd already realized he took his job very seriously.

"Mademoiselle Bailey!" He swished across the lobby in a cloud of expensive cologne, his perfectly polished shoes squeaking slightly against the marble floor. "I hope you are well. All is in good order?"

I loved his grasp of the English language. "Yes, everything is fine, Francois. Thank you."

"May I be of assistance? Do you need any reservations? For a restaurant, perhaps?" His thick accent made him sound not unlike a certain cartoon skunk.

"A cab would be great, thanks."

With an imperious snap of his fingers, Francois sent one of his minions scurrying to hail a black cab. "It is done. 'Ave a truly wondrous day, Mademoiselle Bailey."

With a little wave, I hurried outside.

I had the cabdriver drop me off at the top of a street in North West London. This was it. This used to be *my* street. A couple minutes' walk and I'd be home, back at my flat at the top of the old Edwardian with the tall wooden sash windows that rattled constantly in the wind.

Except that I didn't live there anymore. Not since that night three years ago. After I'd recovered from the attack, Kabita had moved me into her place for a while so she could train me properly. Shortly after that, we'd moved to America, and I'd bought my first house. The little flat in North West London was nothing but a memory.

I closed my eyes and took a deep breath. The air was heavy with damp. It was autumn, and a tiny chill wormed its way beneath my jacket. It had been cold then too. October, and the leaves had crunched under my feet.

As I started down the street, memories came flooding back. The scent of hearth fires mingling with dry leaves, the kiss of the wind on my cheeks, the sound of my footsteps sharp on the pavement.

Something heavy slammed into my left side. I flew through the air, smashing into my neighbor's stonework wall. I actually heard my own ribs snap. The pain made me gag.

I paused. My hands were shaking slightly, and my breath came in quick gasps as pain lanced through my side. It was like I was living it all over again. I pressed my hand to my side, and the phantom pain dissipated.

I realized I was standing next to that very stone wall, the same one that had broken my ribs when I crashed into it. I couldn't help myself. I reached out and placed my palm against the cold stone. Memories flooded back.

My mind struggled to make sense of the fact that I was now lying on the freezing cold ground feeling like I'd been rammed by a truck. Making a little mewling sound in my throat, I groped for my handbag. Everything had spilled out across the pavement. My fingers skittered through lipstick tubes and pens. My phone. Where was it? I needed to call...someone.

I gripped the top of the wall so hard I nearly broke a nail. It was a memory. Just a memory, but I couldn't stop it.

I felt the fangs go right into the jugular. It hurt more than any-thing. The pain ripped through me worse than the broken ribs or the head trauma. I would have screamed, but I had no breath. My hands fluttered against him, trying to beat him off, but I had no strength. His clawed hands squeezed my throat shut, and he slammed my head into the wall again.

The world went black, and there was no more pain and no more blood and no more fear. There was only the sound of my heart beating slower and slower and slower. Then it stopped.

I sucked in a deep breath of cold night air, shoving back the memories and the pain that came with them. As I did, I caught the faintest whiff of something underneath the normal scents of the city.

The truth is that vampires smell no different from people. They retain the same scent in undeath as they carried in life, but my lovely superpowers—which I'd attained thanks to my attack—give me a stronger sense of smell than most people. On top of that was the more metaphysical thing that went along with my other fun Spidey senses—a sort of psychic aroma marking each vamp that goes far beyond a physical odor.

I took another deep breath. There it was again. Very faint, but I knew that scent. I'd never forget it. It was the scent of the vampire who'd killed me.

Still shaking, I made my way farther down the street, follow-ing that faint odor trail. After three years, there wouldn't be any sign of my attacker left. It would have dissipated long ago, which meant he'd been there recently. Hunting.

Only, I am a hunter now too. A smile stretched across my face, and a thrill unfurled in my belly. Deep inside me, the dark-ness began to laugh.

A moment of absolute terror froze me in my tracks. Yes, I love to hunt, but this…This was more. This wasn't me. It was the thing inside me.

With sheer willpower, I managed to shove the feelings away. The ones that weren't mine, but were something entirely alien. The darkness wasn't thrilled about that, but it stayed quiet. For now. I had a feeling it was biding its time. And that was not something I wanted to think about.

I snaked my mobile out of my pocket and dialed Kabita.

"Yes?"

"I'm on the hunt. Just thought you should know."

She hesitated. "Morgan…"

"I have to do this." I hung up, then switched off the phone. I wanted nothing to interfere with this hunt.

As I moved farther down the street, I mentally did a weapons check. I had only one blade. It was strapped to my right ankle. No gun. I did have a garrote hidden in my belt for emergencies. It was the sort that could decapitate a vamp, but it meant I'd have to get in close.

Then there was the special aerosol can. It held an experimental liquid: part holy water, part silver particles, and part salt, meant to work against pretty much every nasty you could think of. The silver was for vamps, the holy water for demons, and the salt for spirits and, sometimes, demons. It is also rumored that salt works on the sidhe, but I had no idea whether that was true or not. I'd never tried the aerosol before, but now was as good a time as any.

I paused in the shadows of the next tree. I could still catch his scent teasing at my nose like a trail of cigarette smoke. Decidedly unpleasant, but also unmistakable. I couldn't feel that itching at the base of my skull, so I knew he wasn't close, but he had been.

I paused in front of the giant wrought-iron gates leading into the "recreation commons." Which is pretty much a snazzy way of saying "park."

The gates were locked, since it was well past sunset. I glanced up and down the shadowy street. The houses were mostly dark, the occasional shaft of light spilling from an open window. I didn't see anyone around, though I could hear the faint *click-click* of high heels on pavement from farther up the street. The sounds were fading, so I figured it was as safe as it was going to get.

The gate was one of those two-sided things that arches up in the middle and then curves down lower at the sides so that, at the edges, it was only a little higher than my head. I gave a little hop and grabbed the crossbar at the top of the gate that was closest to the wall. Using the brick wall for leverage, I scrambled up and onto the top.

I managed to turn around and lower myself down the other side without falling on my head. I leaned up against the wall for a minute to make sure no one had seen me before heading into the park.

I'd never been in the park at night. Even though, vampires aside, the neighborhood is a safe one, it just isn't something a smart girl does. I'd had no idea there isn't any lighting. Probably, it saves energy, but it is incredibly stupid and unsafe since it often gets dark long before the gates are locked.

The deeper I moved into the park, the darker it got. Especially around the pathways where there were large clusters of trees. Still, I couldn't sense any vampires, so I kept moving, following the faint scent of my killer.

It felt a little weird referring to him like that, seeing as I was up and moving around just fine and obviously not dead. But that's exactly what he was—my killer.

About halfway through the park, just as I passed the tennis courts, the scent trail grew a little stronger. I paused to take a deeper breath. Yeah, definitely stronger, but still not a recent trail. It was as though he used this part of the park more often and left his imprint on it.

My palms grew warm and began to itch and tingle. That same feeling of electricity I'd had when I touched the dragon scale. I rubbed them against my jeans, trying to get rid of the strange sensation. It didn't work, so I ignored it and moved on.

Hoops swayed slightly in the breeze, sending eerie shadows dancing across the abandoned basketball court. The chains made the faintest *chink-chink* as the wind tangled them together. I'd never much liked this part of the park. There'd always been lots of teenage boys around, with their saggy jeans and hoodies and aggressive behavior. Maybe it was a stereotype, but like I said, no sense taking chances.

Of course, these days, I face much worse than gangs of teenage hoodies with foul mouths and chips on their shoulders. Not to mention I carry bigger knives.

Up on my right was the entrance to the cemetery. Back home, cemeteries tend to be huge affairs covering several acres. They have posh on-site mortuary services and full-time groundskeepers. In London, cemeteries are usually small, comprising an acre or less. There are no full-time groundskeepers, and mortuary services are usually done in a storefront in town. There are exceptions, of course, like Highgate Cemetery, but generally, the rule holds.

This was an older cemetery, so it was nearly full. There were only a few empty places up near the road, where the groundskeeper's building loomed up out of the darkness.

I'd cut through this particular cemetery more than once back when I lived in London. Though the more superstitious locals tend to steer clear of the place, it is a great shortcut, and I actually quite like cemeteries. They are peaceful and empty, except for the odd necromancer. And they are pretty much harmless guys in robes who have lots of creative ideas about death and magic and very little actual power. Not that I'd known about them back then.

I placed my hand atop one of the granite markers. I knew from memory that most of the markers there were from the 1800s. I wondered vaguely who was buried there, but the vampire's faint scent trail swirled around me. I had no time for reverie.

I approached the groundskeeper's building half expecting to find the trail stopped there, but it continued through the archway that ran through the building and into the courtyard out front. The gravel crunched under my feet as I followed the scent trail across the courtyard and out the front gates of the cemetery.

I found myself standing on the pavement staring up and down the street. I inhaled, trying to catch the scent again. Damn, it was gone.

I backtracked into the courtyard until I picked it up again. It was there, near the archway. I stepped left. Nothing. I stepped right and I caught it. It led me right to the small fenced enclosure, which held a riding mower and a beat-up hearse. The trail stopped there.

That could mean only one thing: the vamp had a ride. There was no way I could track him. He could be anywhere in the city.

∽

I was so glad to get back to my hotel room I collapsed on the bed fully clothed. It was nearly 4:00 a.m., and lack of sleep combined with jet lag was kicking my ass in a big way.

I managed to kick off my boots and shrug out of my jacket, but that was about as far as I got. I snapped off the bedside lamp and curled up in a ball. I was nearly out when my phone rang.

"What?" I snarled at whoever was on the other end.

"Where are you?" *Shit.* It was Jack. That was all I needed. My brain was far too tired to deal with Jack and whatever his deal was. We'd barely spoken since the confrontation we'd had after he'd realized I was royal and decided to make me his personal responsibility, and I wasn't about to start now.

"I'm in bed."

"At eight o'clock at night?"

I sighed. It had taken pretty much all my hunter skills to get out of Portland without him catching on. It hadn't been an easy thing, but obviously I'd succeeded. "I'm in London."

A pause. I could hear the slight hiss and crackle of background noise. "As in England?" His voice was deadly quiet.

"Yes, Jack, as in England. Did you need something?"

"Morgan"—there was anger now—"you should not have left without telling me."

"You're not my dad, Jack. I don't need your permission." That sounded like a whiny teenager, but frankly, I didn't care. It was late. I was tired. And Jack had hurt me more than anyone since Alex, my former fiancé I'd caught cheating on me.

He gave a sigh of exasperation. I could almost see him pinching the bridge of his nose. He does that sometimes when he's trying not to kill me. "If I am to do my job as guardian, I must know where you are. I must be able to protect you."

I wasn't even going to touch that one. Jack and his Atlantean guard duty be damned.

"You should have at least taken the amulet with you," he continued.

Jack wanted me to wear the damn thing ever since I'd activated it, though he wouldn't say why. I, on the other hand, was not about to run around with a piece of ancient Atlantean technology hanging around my neck. Gods knew what it would do to me. It had already messed up my life enough. I was still pretty sure it had something to do with the darkness now living inside of me.

"Jack, I need some sleep. We can talk about this later." Yeah, as in never. This was not an argument I was interested in having.

I hung up before he could say anything else; then I switched the power off. This hanging up on people was turning into a bad habit.

Chapter Six

Slowly, the world shifted from black to white. I realized I had my face smooshed into my pillow and someone was banging on my door. I made one of those embarrassing snorting sounds people sometimes make when they first wake up. There are times I am so grateful I sleep alone.

I managed to haul myself out of bed and stagger to the door. The security lock baffled me for a moment, but I managed to get it open. Thank the gods I was still fully dressed. That could have been embarrassing.

Except, there was no one in the hall. *What the...?*

The knock sounded again. *Shit. Connecting door.* I slammed the hall door and fumbled my way over to the door between Kabita's room and mine.

Kabita eyed me up and down. "You look like crap."

"Gee, thanks." I staggered into the bathroom and saw that, sure enough, I looked like crap.

My skin was pasty, my eyes bloodshot, and my hair looked like a rat had slept in it. As if that weren't bad enough, I hadn't taken off my makeup before going to bed. I had all the sex appeal of a zombie raccoon.

"I need a shower. Can you wait?"

She shrugged and sat down at the desk. "Better make it quick if you want breakfast. Dex is picking us up for the funeral in an hour."

Damn. I'd overslept. "Give me fifteen minutes."

It was more like twenty, but I managed to shower, slap on some makeup, and blow-dry my hair. A couple minutes after that, I was in clean clothes and we were out the door.

I wore a simple black wrap dress that showed off my curves really well, but was still modest enough that I wouldn't look like I was trawling at the funeral. In concession to being a hunter and the weather, I'd opted for my knee-high boots instead of heels, and the few weapons I could hide. I doubted we'd have any trouble of the supernatural variety at the funeral, but one can never be too careful.

Kabita was wearing a formfitting black dress with a black bolero jacket over the top. It looked good on her. Unlike me, she'd bowed to convention with a pair of high heels, even though Kabita's feelings on heels were similar to mine. She must have caught me staring at them, because she gave me a little smile. "Silver alloy knives inside the heels."

"Nice. Did Tessalah work those up?" Tessalah, a freelancer who spent her time inventing all kinds of new tools for dealing with the supernatural, is a freaking genius when it comes to weaponry. I get all my weapons from her and am always happy to give her a hand by trying out prototypes.

"Of course. She's got a really nice line of heels now. You should have a look. There's a killer pair of purple stiletto gladiators."

I practically salivated at that. I am so not a fan of heels, but I would totally make an exception for purple stiletto gladiators. Who wouldn't? Except, since they strap on, they wouldn't be terribly practical as a weapon. Unless Tessalah had found a way around that little problem.

"Where does she hide the blade?"

"Inside the platform. There's a release mechanism in the heel that turns the toe into a lethal weapon," Kabita said.

"I want."

Dex was waiting out front with the car. Kabita slid into the back, so I followed. I figured she could probably use the company.

"Hey, Dex," I said with a little smile. I was tempted to make some kind of stupid joke about him chauffeuring us but figured it was inappropriate.

"Good morning, ladies. You're both looking lovely today." Dex smiled at us in the rearview mirror as he pulled into London traffic.

The ride was a quiet one. I guess we all had things to think about. I imagined Dex and Kabita were thinking about their cousin. I was thinking about Julia too, but for a different reason.

Thanks to the vast number of crime shows on TV these days, it is a pretty well-known fact that murderers often show up at the funerals of their murder victims. Sometimes it's out of guilt, sometimes it's because they like to see the damage they've caused.

I ran my fingers over the smooth scale I'd tucked into the pocket of my dress. If the murderer was really a dragon, did that change things? It wasn't like a dragon could show up at a funeral in broad daylight. Someone was bound to notice. I gave a wry smile at the thought of a giant lizard with wings suddenly appearing in the middle of London.

I still wasn't entirely convinced Julia had been murdered by a dragon. Things just didn't add up. I only hoped Alister didn't go all exterminator. He seemed perfectly happy to blame the dragons, but I knew there had to be more to it.

Dragons. I still couldn't believe they actually still existed. Maybe. It was nuts.

More nuts than a perfectly normal human getting killed by a vampire and waking up with superpowers? my own mind taunted. I ignored that inner voice and went back to rubbing the warmth of the dragon scale between my fingers and staring out the window.

I prefer dealing with the weirdness around me to the weirdness inside me. It's easier that way.

‍ ∽

I recognized the cemetery immediately. No way. "Julia is being buried in Highgate?"

"Of course," Dex said from the front seat. "MI8 always buries their operatives in Highgate. Our family has vaults here too."

Maybe it's macabre of me, but I've always thought the Circle Vaults of Highgate Cemetery are incredibly cool. I'd meant to come on a tour one day, but had never gotten around to it before I left London. It sucked that the only reason I'd made it this time was because someone had died. There was probably a lesson in that.

I turned to Kabita. "You OK?" Stupid question. We were about to attend her cousin's funeral. How could anything be OK?

She shrugged. "It's strange. We'd always been so close, but the last three years, we've struggled to maintain that closeness. We'd e-mail, of course. Pretty regularly. We kept promising we'd take time off and meet up somewhere. But she's been doing her thing, and I've been doing mine. It always seemed like there'd be more time, you know?"

"Yeah." I know better than most just how short life really is.

As we got out of the car, I looped my left arm through her right one. I knew we were both armed, but while she can fight equally well with either hand, I am very right-handed.

"We've got some time before the service. Why don't we take a walk?" I suggested. I figured a walk through the tranquillity of the grounds would do us both some good.

We entered the cemetery arm in arm. It was a beautiful place, full of trees and winding paths, stone archways and vine-covered grave markers. We strolled up the Egyptian Avenue, its tall columns glowing golden in the late-morning sun. It felt like we should be entering a temple at Karnack instead of a cemetery in London.

The light dimmed as we passed under the archway into the long passageway. Though open to the sky, the passage was lined with trees that partially blocked the sun, allowing only a little light to trickle through the leaves.

We kept walking, passing weeping angels wrapped in ivy, vaults cracked with time, crosses lost in vegetation. Highgate Cemetery is old, and it felt every minute of its age. I absolutely loved it.

"So, what's the deal with you and your dad?" When in doubt, bluntness works.

Kabita's arm tensed in mine. Then she shrugged and heaved a sigh. "You probably noticed we don't exactly get along."

"Yeah." My tone was wry. "I definitely noticed that. Has it always been that way with you two?"

"Pretty much. I mean, it was OK when I was younger. I didn't see much of him. Mom hated London. Still does. So she stayed in Malaysia and raised us while Dad stayed in London. He'd come out two or three times a year to visit. Bring us presents and tell us stories of his adventures with MI8."

"Your mom knew about MI8 and all the monster stuff?" I asked in amazement. It isn't something that gets tossed about much. My mom definitely doesn't know about the monster stuff. She certainly doesn't know what I do for a living, and I plan on keeping it that way. The very thought of her finding out makes me shudder in horror.

"Yeah. Her family and Dad's have been tied together for generations. My mother is a Gupta. Gupta, in Hindi, means 'protector.'"

Seriously cool. "Your mother's family is hunters?"

"That is one of their functions, yes. My mother's family moved from India to Malaysia when the native hunters were wiped out during a plague. The islands needed new hunters, and the Guptas were the best."

"And your father? How did he and your mother end up together?"

She paused in front of a grave marker. The marble had been carved to look like a woman sleeping on plush cushions, her beautiful face peaceful. Age had worn the edges soft, making her look almost real.

"Their families agreed to join forces, so to speak. Unusual for an Englishman, I know, but I guess they hoped that a Jones and a Gupta would create a superhunter of sorts."

I must have looked surprised, because she laughed. "I know. It's ridiculous."

"So they had an arranged marriage?" The concept was pretty alien to most Western minds, but during my time in London, I'd known many people in arranged marriages. It surprised me that a white British man would have agreed to one, though.

"In a way. It was actually my father's idea." Kabita scowled. "Being aligned with the Guptas made the Jones family incredibly popular and powerful among many of the other hunter families. And my father loves nothing so much as power."

"Did it work? Did they turn out a superhunter?"

She shook her head. "No. None of us are super anything. My brothers hunt, but none of them are natural born. And me..." Her voice trailed off.

I frowned. "What about you?" I knew she isn't a hunter in the same way I am. Even though my superabilities had come to me because of the vampire attack, I am considered a natural—someone born with hunter skills—because of my ability to sense the vampires. Though she is damn good at hunting down demons, she can't actually sense them.

"It backfired. I was born a natural, but not a natural hunter. I was born a natural witch."

I already knew she was a natural witch, so that didn't come as a surprise, but her comment about the backfire sure did. "What do you mean? Don't witches run in your family?" That is the usual way. It is rare for a natural witch to be born to a nonwitch family.

Her face hardened, and she continued down the path, pulling me along with her. "No. Maybe. I don't know. What I do know is that the Joneses were instrumental during many of the witch trials in England and pushed for so many of the witches to be hanged. They were the ones who set up the charter preventing witches, whether natural born or religious, from joining MI8. And they're still trying to persecute witches today. My father is their driving force."

Holy crap. "But there are loads of witches in the UK," I pointed out.

"Wiccans, not true witches. They follow a religion, a spiritual path. They are not born with the power of a natural witch. True witches are very rare. I only started showing the signs after I turned thirteen. Everything changed with my father after that."

Interesting. I hadn't known that. "So your father hates what you are." It was harsh, but it was what it was.

"Yes."

"Shit. That sucks." I'd seen how cold Alister had been toward her, so I wasn't entirely surprised.

Her smile was wry. "Oh, yes. Big-time."

I squeezed her arm and drew her farther down the path. "Well, I love you, and I think you're amazing."

She grinned. "I love you too, but let's not get too mushy, all right?"

I laughed.

The sun shining through the branches of the trees dappled our skin and warmed our heads. It was so nice out I almost wished I'd worn sandals instead of boots.

"Anyway, Mom wasn't about to let Dad haul me off and lock me up or have me exorcised or something, so she sent me to live with my aunt in London. She is a very powerful member of the board of directors of MI8, and she doesn't have the Jones prejudice against witches. She hasn't been active in years, but she trained me, taught me everything she knows. She couldn't get me into MI8, but she made sure I had everything I needed to do my job and become respected in my own right."

"I take it she was the one who helped you get me out of MI8 custody?"

"Yes." Kabita nodded. "She's an amazing woman."

"What's your aunt's name? I'd like to thank her."

She smiled a little at that. "I'm sure she'd love to meet you. She'll be there today. Her name is Angeline Reynolds. She's Julia's mother."

After a leisurely walk, we finally arrived at the Jones family vault where Julia would be interred.

I guess I've always had a hard time fearing death. Maybe because I live with it every day. Maybe because I've been dead. Or maybe because, to me, death isn't the end, but a transition. At least, that is what it has always felt like.

Even before my attack, when everything changed, I viewed death more as a temporary state than something real and lasting. Probably not the healthiest attitude for a teenage girl, but what can you do? I've never exactly been normal.

There were about a dozen people standing in front of the vault. Of course I recognized Alister and Dex Jones straightaway. There were two other men, younger than Dex but nearly identical to him. It was pretty obvious they were Kabita's other brothers, Adam and Adler.

The twins greeted us with warm hugs. Obviously, they didn't share their father's prejudice against Kabita.

There were also a couple of desk jockey types, a man and a woman, looking a little nervous around the Jones family. Kabita pointed them out as Julia's coworkers at MI8. I eyed them both. They had worked in the same office as Julia, which meant they could have some idea about whatever it was she'd stumbled across that led to her murder. And that meant they were suspects, despite the dragon scale in my purse that might say otherwise.

The man was thin and close to six foot four, with that slight hunch that tall people sometimes have, like they are embarrassed of their height. His thin brown hair was badly in need of a trim, and his white dress shirt and black trousers were a little rumpled, like maybe he'd been working all night and hadn't changed.

The woman, on the other hand, was neat as a pin. If she'd worn her hair down, it probably would have been a thick, frizzy mass, but she wore it pinned into a severe bun, almost hiding the fact that it was just this side of ginger. Her nose was a little too long and her face a little too narrow to be pretty, but she was interesting. The round wire-rimmed glasses perched on her nose were several years out of date and, combined with her neatly pressed black skirt suit, made her look like a librarian or a schoolmarm.

Frankly, they both looked harmless, but I've learned over the years that looks can be very deceiving. I wouldn't write those two off the suspect list quite yet. Besides, they worked for MI8, and when spooks were involved, even desk jockeys could be dangerous.

Kabita led me over to another woman standing by herself at the front of the little group. She was slightly built and on the short side, but she stood ramrod straight, her blonde bob topped with a chic little black hat, a wisp of netting partially covering her face.

It was a pretty face. She reminded me a lot of the picture I'd seen of Julia, but older.

"Aunt Angeline, this is my friend Morgan Bailey. She's the hunter you helped me save."

"I remember." Angeline Reynolds held out a dainty hand. My hands were not big, but they dwarfed those of Kabita's aunt. Her skin was warm and soft, and I sensed strength in her.

"Mrs. Reynolds, I'm very sorry for your loss."

She gave me a gracious nod. "Thank you, Miss Bailey. Welcome back to London." Her voice was cultured, her clothes expensive, and the very faint whiff of her perfume exquisite. This was one classy lady. She didn't deserve the kind of sorrow I saw etched into her face. No one deserves to suffer the loss of a child. Especially not like this. And especially not the woman who'd made sure I'd had a second chance at life.

I kept hold of her hand and stepped a little closer than was entirely polite. Lowering my voice, I whispered, "I want to assure you, Mrs. Reynolds, that I will bring Julia's killer to justice. I don't care who or what that killer may be. I will not stop until it is done. I promise."

Her blue eyes, identical to those I'd see in the picture of her daughter, gazed at me from underneath the black netting of her hat. For a long moment, she said nothing. And then all she said was, "Thank you."

Chapter Seven

As funerals went, it was a pleasant enough one. The Anglican priest read some scriptures and said a few prayers, the usual fare about ashes to ashes and so forth. Alister made a short speech about how deeply Julia had touched those around her and what a loss she'd be to the world. Julia's female coworker said some nice things about how Julia had been a good person and lovely to work with, stuff like that. Then she started talking about their "girls' nights" and how Julia had supported her during the breakup of her marriage, and next thing you knew she was sobbing her way through a box of tissues. There were several hankies out. Julia Reynolds may not have been close to a lot of people, but she obviously mattered to those who counted her as a friend.

At the end of the service, her mother stepped forward and laid a pink rose on the coffin. She stood there quietly for a moment, as though she could communicate with her daughter. Maybe she could. I've seen weirder things.

One by one, all the other attendees took a pink rose from a nearby vase and laid it on the coffin. Except for the tall man who'd been Julia's coworker. He waited until everyone was finished; then, instead of a rose, he laid a single black-eyed Susan, which he'd been holding throughout the service, on top of the roses.

When he looked up, I caught his eye. There was such loss there that, for a moment, it took my breath away. Then he moved on, shoulders slumped. I realized then that he wasn't ashamed of his height. He was simply weighed down by sadness. "He loved her," I whispered to Kabita. "He really loved her."

Kabita looked down at the solitary orange flower among the sea of pink. The colors clashed, but strangely, it worked.

"Susans were her favorite, you know. She particularly liked the orange ones. She told me once they made her think of sunshine and summer. You're right; he must have loved her. I wonder if he ever told her?"

The thought that he might not have made me feel incredibly sad. I'd be the first to admit that life is short, at least for most people. And while my love life is certainly no shining example, at least I have no regrets.

Well, maybe one. But the situation with Jack was beyond my control. Another man crept into my thoughts. I shook my head. Inigo was a matter for another time.

As we turned to follow the others back to the car park, something flickered at the corner of my vision. I turned my head. Nothing. I frowned.

I grabbed Kabita's arm and pulled her back into the shadow of a large tree. "I think someone's watching us."

Both of us scanned the grounds. "There," she whispered, "over by that vault with the giant cross on top."

Sure enough, someone was hiding behind the vault. I could just see part of the person's head and a flutter of cloth from a jacket or something. "I think it's the woman from the airport. You know, the one who looked at you funny?"

"How on earth can you tell that from this distance?" She squinted a little as if to see better, but the woman had dodged back behind the vault.

"Spiky platinum-blonde hair. Right height. Right shape. Definitely a woman and definitely an unusual hair color." I slid around to the other side of the tree so I'd be out of the woman's direct line of vision. "I'm going after her. I want to find out what she wants."

"OK. I'll keep her attention on me." Kabita peered around the tree, making herself just obvious enough to be seen by the other woman, but hopefully not so obvious our little spy would catch on.

I nodded and moved out quietly from the tree. From this angle, the woman couldn't see me, as the large stone vault with its oversize cross blocked her view. Unfortunately, that meant I couldn't see her, either.

I made my way as quickly and quietly as I could toward the vault, but I must not have been quiet enough. As I rounded the vault, the woman started, and I got a good look at her face. It was definitely the woman from the airport. What on earth was she doing there at the cemetery?

She took off running.

"Hey, stop!" I took off after her. She darted down one of the pathways that led deeper into the grounds. This part of the grounds was extremely overgrown and the woman kept disappearing from view, only to reappear farther down the path.

Silently urging my feet to go faster, I followed her down a particularly overrun path. No such luck. Instead of speeding up, I tripped on an exposed root and nearly went sprawling face-first into the dirt path. I managed to catch myself, but the woman had vanished.

Leaning up against a nearby tree, I paused to catch my breath, see if I could spot her. There was a flash of silvery white through the trees. I took off running again, this time keeping a closer eye out for sneaky roots.

I rounded a bend in the path just in time to see the blonde woman exit the parklands and hop into a waiting car. It took off with a squeal of tires, leaving streaks of black behind it. *Show-off.*

With a groan, I bent over to catch my breath. As I did, I caught a familiar scent. It was the same one I'd caught the night before. The scent of the vampire who'd killed me.

I straightened, inhaling deeply. There it was again. But strangely, it was only the physical odor, like anyone would smell from another human. There was no accompanying metaphysical scent that I could sense with my enhanced hunter abilities.

I moved along the path a little farther until it forked. The smell was stronger down the left fork, which led deeper into the parklands of the cemetery, disappearing inside a large grove of trees. Left it was.

Color me suspicious, but I found it strange that the vampire scent had shown up in the same place as the mysterious woman from the airport. I didn't know what that meant, but I sure as heck meant to find out.

The smell got stronger as I moved along the path, so strong I almost gagged. He was there. He had to be. There was no way the scent could be that strong without the vampire being very close by. I knew Kabita was waiting for me, but I couldn't resist. I needed to follow that trail.

I picked up my pace, jogging past rows of gravestones tilted at crazy angles and statues spattered with bird droppings. Something niggled at me. I couldn't sense the vampire. I could smell him, but that was a physical thing. My abilities had nothing to do with the physical. I couldn't understand why I could smell him so strongly, but I couldn't *feel* him. If he was so close, I should have had that whole tingly scalp pressure thing going on. Maybe my vamp radar was on the fritz.

I shoved the thought aside and kept going, following the scent trail through the park, under trees and beneath archways. It led me straight to the Circle Vaults.

The vaults looked exactly as they did on the countless documentaries I'd watched on TV. I hurried down the wide steps to the underground level. The Circle Vaults reminded me a little of the catacombs under the ruins of the Colosseum in Rome. All those little rooms on either side of a wide hallway exposed to the elements. I could almost imagine there had once been a floor above them now rotted away, but they'd been built like that. It was an odd place for a vampire to hide. Unless he'd made it into one of the locked vaults. The heavy oak doors were all locked, though, so he would have needed a key.

The scent led me past door after ancient door before dead ending in front of one marked *Sanford*. The door was thick oak bound with iron, and older than dirt. I tried the handle, but it didn't budge. The vault was locked up tight.

"Shit!" Probably not an appropriate sentiment for a cemetery, but I was pissed off. He was in there. Even though I still couldn't feel him, he *had* to be in there. I couldn't think of any other explanation.

I yanked at the door again. As though that would do any good. It didn't. I could feel the anger and annoyance boiling just below the surface; fortunately, I had a good grip on the darkness, but my hands felt itchy and tight. Fury rode me, setting the blood throbbing in my temples. I let out a scream of frustration and slapped my palm against the wood.

Then I jumped back with a yelp as the door burst into flames.

I staggered back, mouth hanging open. I must have looked like a fish. Real attractive. But honestly, it isn't every day you see a door burst into flames for no apparent reason.

Except, perhaps, that I touched it.

The fire ate at the hard oak, blackening the wood and sending thick smoke spiraling skyward. Shouting in the distance told me it was time to make myself scarce. I was pretty sure I'd get the blame, and how on earth was I going to explain the fact that I'd just set a door on fire without the aid of matches or a lighter?

No, that was ridiculous. It couldn't have been me. I couldn't have set the door on fire with nothing more than my touch. The very idea was absurd.

As absurd as a woman who could channel the power of darkness.

Something sparked in the back of my mind. A conversation I'd once had with Eddie Mulligan back in his shop in Portland. We'd been talking about my ability to channel darkness, and he'd mentioned that, once, there had been people who could channel other elements.

Elements like fire.

"Oh crap," I whispered. "Oh, this is not good."

I hurried back down the path toward where I'd left Kabita. She was still there, leaning against a tree. "No joy?"

"No. She had a car waiting." I rubbed my palms against my thighs, trying to keep them from trembling. I didn't mention the fire thing to Kabita. I was just way too freaked out. I didn't want to think about it, let alone talk about it. I wanted to pretend it never happened.

Kabita sighed. "Too bad. I wonder what she wanted."

"Couldn't have been good, her spying on us like that."

She shrugged and headed toward the parking lot. "Don't jump to conclusions. There were more than a couple MI8 agents at the funeral today. She might have been watching any one of them."

But I knew she was wrong. That woman had been there to watch us. Or more likely, based on what I'd seen at the airport, she'd been there to watch Kabita.

"Dad's throwing a wake back at his flat in Belgravia. I figured we could pop in for a while." I couldn't tell from her tone whether she had any interest in attending or not.

I shook my head. "I really need to head back to the hotel, do some research. And I need to call Eddie."

Kabita gave me a look. "It's four thirty in the morning back home. I don't think he'd appreciate your calling at that time of morning."

Good point. I hadn't even thought about the eight-hour time difference. I sighed. "Fine. I really do need to do some research, though, so I don't want to stay too long."

"Don't worry"—Kabita gave me one of her mysterious smiles—"you'll be amazed at how much research you can get done at one of these things."

∽

"Morgan, this is Sandra Fuentes, dragon artist." Kabita grinned at me like a lunatic as she led me out onto the terrace. Which meant she was about to introduce me to someone who was going to rock my world and she secretly thought it was hilarious.

"Dragon artist?"

The woman in front of me was willow thin and ghostly pale. Even her gray eyes were pale to the point of nearly being color-less. The only bit of color was her hair. The straight, silky mass fell nearly to her waist and shone rich blue-black in the sun.

Her grip, as she shook my hand, was surprisingly strong. Her skin gave off a slight spark. That static electricity again. I was feeling way too much of it lately.

"Morgan Bailey, lovely to meet you at last. My sister has told me so much about you."

I glanced from Sandra to Kabita. "Your sister?"

"Sandra is Cordelia Nightwing's twin sister," Kabita told me with a grin. Cordelia is a clairvoyant and a friend of mine. She's helped me a lot over the years.

I must have looked absolutely gobsmacked, because Sandra let out a belly laugh. "She didn't tell you a thing about me, did she? Isn't that just like Cordy? The woman always did live halfway in another world." Her accent was definitely American, though she slipped a few British pronunciations in here and there, much like I'd done when I lived there.

61

"Um, no. No, she didn't. I mean, she mentioned once that she had a sister, but she never told me anything else. It's nice to meet you, Sandra." Obviously, they weren't identical twins, though there were some similarities now that I knew they were related.

"I see Adam. Listen, I'll leave you two to chat. Enjoy." Kabita headed off to catch up with her brother as Sandra waved me toward a couple of chairs overlooking the communal gardens.

"So, what exactly is a dragon artist?" OK, stupid question, but I never said I was a scintillating conversationalist.

She graciously ignored my idiocy. "I make dragons. Statues, carvings, that sort of thing. Surprising amount of money in dragons. People like them. Little clay ones are the most popular. Great for desks and such. Sell a ton of those. Though I make a pretty penny off big stone ones for the garden. Unbelievable how many people want a dragon in their back garden. Certainly better than those ugly gnome things."

"So, you're a sculptor."

She smiled. "Well, yes, you could say that. Sculptor, yes. I like that."

I blinked. Good lord, the woman was odd. "So, how long have you been sculpting dragons?" I took a sip of the cold lemonade I'd been handed when we arrived. It tasted more like Sprite, but that's British lemonade for you.

"Oh, all my life," she said with an airy wave of her hand. "I just found it came so naturally to me."

"You didn't go to art school or something? Maybe get a set of sculpting tools when you were a kid?"

She looked surprised. "Why, no. Why would I use tools?"

"Um, because that's how you make a statue from clay or stone." I said it slowly, like I was talking to someone really thick.

"Oh, goodness me." She laughed. "I don't need tools for that. Here, watch!" She leaned over and grabbed a smooth stone about the size of my palm from the planter next to us and placed it on the table, her palm lightly covering the stone. She closed her eyes and whispered something under her breath, then lifted her hand.

"Oh my gods." Sitting on the table where the rock had been was a perfectly carved statuette of a dragon midflight. Every little detail was intricately etched, right down to its slightly irregular scales and the veins running through its wings. I might have thought it was real if I didn't know it was stone.

"I know, isn't it cool?" Her voice held more than just a hint of amusement. I think maybe she was laughing at me.

Chapter Eight

I think we have much to talk about, don't you?" Sandra leaned forward and placed her hand gently over mine. Her skin was warm, much warmer than it should have been. I wondered whether she was running a temperature or something. It made me think of Inigo all of a sudden. He is always a little warm too. Then there was that zing I got from her. That almost electrical spark of energy, which I also get from Inigo, but for entirely different reasons. With Inigo, the zing is attraction. With Sandra, it was something lighter, more superficial.

"Yeah. Yeah, we do." I subtly rubbed at my hand, easing away the feeling.

She leaned back in her seat, the sun picking out the blue highlights in her hair. "Then why don't you come visit me at my shop tomorrow? We can talk more freely then." She fished around in her handbag and brought out a business card that was slightly the worse for wear. "I'm over in Soho. Such a delightful place, don't you think? Quite a lot of tourists, but the atmosphere makes up for it."

I'd been to Soho a few times back when I lived in London. She was right. It is a fantastic place full of life and vibrancy. It is also quite an eye-opener. Soho is like a mini San Francisco with a side order of Amsterdam thrown in for good measure.

I took the card she offered. "Tomorrow. Sure. I'll be there." The investigation would no doubt take a few more days, and I just had a feeling Sandra was going to come in handy.

"Very good." She gathered her things and stood up. "Well, I'm off. It was lovely to meet you, Morgan. I'll be seeing you tomorrow." The corners of her eyes crinkled as she smiled.

I couldn't help but smile back, even though I was feeling a bit *Alice in Wonderland* at the moment. A woman who could turn stone into dragons with the touch of a hand? Talk about one giant rabbit hole.

I stared at her retreating form, bemused, as she disappeared behind the other mourners milling about on the terrace. Every time I thought I had things figured out, they got weirder.

"Come on." Kabita popped out of nowhere. "I've called a cab. I need a pub."

"I'll second that."

The black cab dropped us off not far from our hotel. The Audley was a classic British pub just blocks from the American embassy; it had a long, polished wood bar, heavy oak-beamed ceilings, and antique plateglass windows. Kabita ordered drinks at the bar, and we settled in at one of the little tables looking out onto Mount Street.

It was a weekday and just after the lunch-hour rush, so the pub was dim and quiet. Suited me fine.

"So, what do you think of Sandra?" Kabita grinned.

"She's…odd. Do you know what she can do with a rock?" I took a big gulp of pear cider.

She nodded. "Yeah. I did a background on Cordelia when you first met her and discovered she had a sister here in London. The report said she had some magical talent. It did *not* say that she used that talent to make dragon statues." She shook her head. "Can you imagine the guys at MI8 trying to figure out that one?"

I laughed. "Bet that baffled them for a day or two. I wonder why Cordy never talks about her sister?"

She shrugged. "Who knows? Maybe they don't get along. Or maybe she just couldn't figure out how to say, 'Hey, I've got a sister who turns rocks into dragon sculptures using magic.' Not something that comes up in normal conversation."

I supposed she was right. I don't exactly go around telling people my father died before I was born and my mother tried to channel Martha Stewart on a daily basis. And, no, I don't mean literally channel. "I've been wondering about something."

She glanced over at me. "Yeah?"

"Why won't MI8 let witches join? I mean, I know you said your family had a lot to do with that. But why do they hate them so much? And why, in the twenty-first freaking century, are they still such bigots? For goodness' sake, MI8 is as much about protecting nondangerous supernaturals from extinction as they are about protecting the human population from the dangerous ones. The witch thing seems a little odd."

She sighed, fingers toying with the straw in her glass. "You know as well as I do that there's still a lot of prejudice in the world. Particularly when it comes to bureaucracy, and Europe is a lot worse about bureaucracy than the Americas. And they hold on to their prejudices for generations."

"Yeah, OK. So?"

"So, MI8 is convinced that witches, particularly natural witches, are dangerous and prone to go over to 'the dark side,' for lack of a better term. They've seen a lot of witches go bad, wanting more and more power until they drown in it. It's not the power itself that is bad, any more than a gun is inherently bad. It's what it does to the user. You know what they say about power."

Of course I do. Everyone does. "Power corrupts. And absolute power corrupts absolutely." Trite but true.

Kabita took a sip of her drink. "Exactly. Now, imagine you not only are already naturally powerful, but have the ability to grow your power exponentially by pulling power from the earth and the universe. So much power you're drunk with it. Imagine what that could do to a person."

"We all have that ability. Every single human being. Anyone can do that with practice."

Her expression grew tight. "But what if you could pull the energy from other people to fuel your own? To literally have the power of life and death."

I felt the muscles in my shoulders tighten. I didn't have to imagine. I knew. The darkness shifted inside me, wanting out—and beside it, I felt something new. Something hot and bright and hungry. My hands started doing that tingly thing again.

I struggled with panic even as I struggled with the darkness. *Not here. Not now.*

"Are you OK?" Kabita had obviously noticed something was wrong.

"Yeah, I'm fine." But my voice came out a little strained.

It was a struggle, but I shoved the darkness down along with whatever that new thing was, slamming the metaphorical lid on it as fast as I could. My hands clenched my glass until my knuckles turned white. No, I didn't have to imagine at all.

"Are you saying you have that ability?" I asked Kabita. She'd never mentioned it before, and I couldn't blame her. The very idea was terrifying.

She was silent a moment. "I don't know. But in theory, yes, I do. All natural witches do. It would take a very strong person to resist the pull of that power," she continued. "And most of us just aren't that strong. That sort of power exploits every fear, every weakness. After a while, it can't be controlled anymore. Even a good witch goes bad eventually." She took another sip of her drink before placing it carefully back on the scarred wood table. "At least, that's what MI8 says."

Was Kabita talking about herself? Or me?

"Is that what your father told them?"

She nodded. "Yes. It's what his family has believed for generations. I come from a long line of witch hunters."

I shook my head. "I still can't get over that."

"Ironic, isn't it? The very first Jones—Jonas—was an orphan, raised by the Church. Originally, they raised him to be an ordinary hunter, but things changed by the time he came of age." She took another long drink.

Kabita, the witch, descended from witch hunters. Irony wasn't the half of it.

"The Church was having problems maintaining its control over England at the time," she continued. "All these pesky women trying to get the locals to *think* rather than blindly accept whatever the Church told them. So, instead of sending Jonas to fight demon spawn and vampires and whatnot, they sent him to hunt down and murder witches."

My eyes must have been as big as saucers. I took a big gulp of my drink. "Hooo, boy. That's a bit out there. Can't say I'm surprised, though."

"No," she agreed. "The Church has a lot of sins to answer for."

"And Jonas? What happened to him?"

"He was good at his job. Really good. The Church wanted him to marry, produce heirs to be raised as witch hunters like their sire. The witches, on the other hand, wanted no such thing. They knew that Jonas's ability to hunt was more than just a matter of good training. It was more in the realm of the supernatural."

"He was a natural-born hunter?" I asked.

She nodded the affirmative. "Probably a demon hunter or something similar. It would explain why my brothers and I are so good at it, but the Church refused to acknowledge it. It retrained him to use his abilities against witches. Something the witches figured out. So they sent one of their own, a young woman named Ysoria, to pose as a virtuous young woman of the Church and seduce him, marry him, in order to prevent his children from being trained by the Church as well."

"I'm guessing it worked." *Damn.* This was like something out of a really bad sci-fi movie.

"Yeah," she said. "It worked. She was supposed to kill any children they had so there would be no one for the Church to train. There would be other people, but a natural hunter is rare, and that's what they were worried about. Especially since the Church had its claws in Jonas."

"She obviously didn't do it, or you wouldn't be sitting here today, Kabita Jones."

"Ysoria moved in with her blood sister—a nonwitch—using the excuse that Jonas was gone hunting so often she felt unsafe alone. When Jonas was away, the two women pretended the children belonged to the sister. Ysoria had just had her third child when the witches discovered her deceit. They killed the older children, but she hid the baby. When Jonas discovered that she was a witch and that her coven had murdered their children, he killed her."

"Shit."

"I know." Her smile was a bit weak. "Jonas took the baby to the Church for the monks to raised and then disappeared."

"And he never told the Church his wife was a witch?"

"No. Can you imagine?"

"So how do you know all this?"

"He killed the woman anyway and eventually returned to the Church. He never told them of his heritage but spent the rest of his life trying to purge himself of 'sin,' as he called it." Her voice dripped with disdain. "He trained his own children to hate and fear witches and to ignore any abilities that might crop up. Each generation followed suit, denying their heritage and decrying it as evil."

I leaned back against the hard bench, shifting to get comfortable. *Shit.* That was fucked up. "Until you."

"Yes, until me. My mother's people do not share European views on witches. Quite the opposite, in fact. My mother refused to allow my father to repress me or my abilities. Instead, she had me properly trained."

"And so the witch hunter's son has a witch for a daughter." I snorted. "Ah, the irony."

"Trust me, the irony is not lost on my father; he simply isn't amused by it."

I downed the last of my drink. "Obviously, the man needs to work on his sense of humor."

She laughed. "Obviously."

We were headed out the door when I caught sight of a woman on the other side of the street. I stopped abruptly, causing Kabita to crash into me. "What the—" she said, but I shushed her.

"Look. It's her! The woman from the airport." I pointed down the street. A woman with spiky platinum-blonde hair was striding along the pavement, her black leather boots making a clicking sound that echoed off the old brick buildings on either side of the street.

"Morgan—" Kabita started to say something, but I ignored her. I was going to catch that woman and make her tell me why she was following us.

I took off down the street at a dead run. The woman must have heard me coming, but she didn't turn; instead, she kept walking, her hips doing that little sashay thing women do when they're wearing heels.

I grabbed her by the arm, spinning her around. She shrieked, pulling away from me. "Get away from me! Stop or I'll scream!" She held her handbag in front of her like a shield.

"Oh, gods, I'm sorry. I thought you were someone else." I lifted my hands up and backed slowly away. It wasn't her. This girl was much younger than the woman from the airport. She looked like she was still in her teens, and had a bright-pink streak through her bangs. She was shorter too, up close. She'd had her earbuds in, which was why she hadn't heard me. "I'm really, really sorry."

She scurried off, casting a frightened look behind her. Poor kid would probably be scarred for life. *Crap.*

"Good one, Morgan." I hadn't heard Kabita come up behind me.

"Hey, I thought it was her, OK? Sure looked like it from behind."

"You need to slow down. I know you have a lot on your plate right now and finding this woman is important to you, not to mention taking care of that vampire, but you can't go around accosting innocent people on the street."

Her comment pissed me off, but she wasn't wrong. I'd been running around like a headless chicken, and I hadn't had much luck finding either of the people in question. I guess I was angrier with myself than anything. I turned and, without a word, headed for the hotel, Kabita trailing behind.

By the time we got back to the hotel it was late enough to call Eddie. But before we could get to our rooms, we were accosted by Francois.

"Mademoiselle Bailey! Mademoiselle Jones! 'Ow was your day? Is there anything I can do for you? You need some room service? Some fresh towels? Anything you want, I can get for you! It is my responsibility to see that everything is perfect for you." He finished his sentence with a flourish of hands.

We assured him we were fine and managed to escape to the elevator intact. But it was a close call. I left Kabita at her door and went next door to my own room.

I used my mobile, since Inigo, the techno-genius, had rigged it so it couldn't be bugged or traced. I really needed to talk to Eddie about the fire business, and I didn't want the wrong people overhearing.

Unfortunately, it made no difference. Eddie didn't answer. Probably up in the attic again.

I decided to get some sleep and try him later. The events of the last couple of days combined with some serious jet lag were taking their toll.

I closed my eyes and let sleep suck me under. For the first time since I'd touched the Key of Atlantis, a dream was waiting.

Chapter Nine

The spray of salty water lashed my face, ice cold soaking through the thin cloth of my dress. I hadn't bothered to grab my cloak. The rage had been too much, blinding me to all else.

I burned with hunger. To devour. To destroy.

Below me, the sea crashed against the rocks, sending another icy spray over me. Still, it did nothing to dispel the rage burning through me, turning my bones to fire.

"Fina! Fina!"

His voice called to me, even against the roar of the ocean. I turned. He stood, kissed by moonlight, glowing like a messenger of the gods. Part of me loved him so much it hurt. And part of me wanted to rend him in two. "Stop, Iah. Stop."

"Fina, please," he begged. So beautiful in the moonlight, his golden hair like spun silver danced across a face that would make a sculptor weep. So beautiful he made my heart ache. "Fina, please don't do this. There has to be another way."

"There isn't." My heart was breaking, but there was no other choice. I'd become a danger to everyone and everything I loved. "I cannot control myself any longer." I daren't tell him how much I wanted to lose control. "The fire—it burns, Iah. It wants to burn everything." The tears that dripped down my face were scalding hot and mixed with the cold spray of the ocean.

"Please, Fina, please." But his tone told me he'd already given up. He knew I was right.

My heart wept. Now, at last, I couldn't even hold him, though my fingers ached to caress his moon-touched skin one last time. Iah, the first male in our history born with the power of the moon. There hadn't even been a name for him in our language. The priests had searched the scrolls for months to find a suitable name for him in the language of the ancients.

"Iah," I breathed.

Tears trickled down his face. I'd never seen him cry before. My heart would have broken then if it hadn't already been shattered to pieces.

"I love you, Iah. With all that I am and all that I will ever be. I swear this, one day, in another life, we will be together."

I turned back to the sea far beneath me. Perhaps the fire would be quenched in her chilly depths, but the most important thing was that the water would stop the fire from destroying anyone else. It would stop me from giving in. Pain screamed through me, and I swayed. Only sheer determination kept me upright. "From fire I was born and to fire I return."

I looked behind me one last time. Iah had sunk to his knees, his body racked with sobs. But I had no choice. If I didn't do this now, the fire would burn through me and take everyone with it. It was the curse of the fire kissed.

The sea beckoned, so before I could talk myself out of it, I threw myself from the cliff. The fire within me screamed and burned, angry that I'd denied it, but I would soon be free. Wind streamed past my face, tearing my eyes. The water loomed closer.

A great beast swooped from the shadows. "Dracona," I breathed. My lifelong friend and companion. The water would not take me, after all.

"Fire bringer," she whispered back.

For just one moment, I saw in her eyes infinite sorrow, and then her mighty jaw opened. Flame shot from her throat.

I burned.

∽

I came awake with a start, thrashing at the duvet, barely holding back a scream. It took me a minute to figure out I wasn't on fire, though I was drenched in sweat and stinking of nightmares.

I pressed my palm against my chest, willing my heart to slow. The palm of my hand was hot, and I jerked it away from my skin, leaving a pink print behind on my chest.

Shakily, I stumbled out of bed and into the bathroom and splashed water on my face, trying to shake the horrific dream. "Gods, what the hell was that?"

It had been weeks since I'd had one of my dreams. When I first started hunting for the missing amulet of Atlantis, I started having these crazy dreams. Except, it had turned out they weren't dreams at all but glimpses into the ancient past. I'd thought that, with the whole discovery of the amulet and me being the Key of Atlantis thing, the dreams would have stopped. Apparently not. The amulet must have decided it had more to tell me, despite the fact that I was several thousand miles away. Either that or I was getting dreams from the dragon scale now.

I checked the time—3:00 a.m. It was still early evening back home, so I dialed Eddie again. If anyone would know what the dream meant, it would be him.

He picked up on the third ring.

"Hey, Eddie."

"Morgan Bailey! I knew it must be you. How is London? Have you seen the queen? What about Prince William? Isn't he a handsome one? I did so love his mother—"

"Eddie!" I broke in. He'd go on like that for an hour if I'd let him. "No, no queen, no prince. I haven't seen any famous people at all."

"Ah, well. One can dream. So I imagine you didn't call to give me a status report on the royals?"

I laughed at that. "Uh, no. I rang because, well…" How to say it? I mean, it sounded so crazy, even to me.

"Morgan, what's wrong?"

I told him everything—about Julia and her murder, the blonde woman from the airport, and the cemetery. Then I told him about scenting the vampire—my murderer, of sorts—and about following him. Finally, I told him about the fire.

He was quiet for a moment. "Morgan, this isn't good. I mean, chasing that vampire around the city like a lunatic. And that woman."

"Eddie, I get it. I sound like a basket case. But I'm a little more concerned about this fire business. I mean, I set a freaking door on fire!"

"Yes, yes, I know. It is worrying."

"Yeah, worrying would be the word for it. I'm spouting flames out my fingertips." Not literally, of course. I still wasn't 100 percent sure it was my touch that started the fire at the vaults, but things were leaning in that direction. I started pacing back and forth across my room. There wasn't much space, so it was a short walk.

"First it was the kissing darkness business, and now fire. It's just so strange. Have you come into contact with anything unusual recently?"

"Now that you mention it"—I rubbed my fingers across the dragon's scale, which I'd taken out of my purse and laid on the desk, and once again, I noticed it felt strangely warm to the touch—"I was given a dragon's scale."

He let out a little squeak. "A dragon's scale? Oh my goodness! But dragons are extinct."

"Apparently not. I think someone is trying to frame them for Julia Reynolds's murder." I hadn't put that thought into words until just then, but it made sense.

"And someone gave you a dragon scale? As in, you touched it? Physically?"

"Yes," I told him. "I'm holding it right now."

"Oh my. Oh, my, my. Well, that explains it."

"Explains what, exactly?"

"Well, it *sort* of explains it."

"Eddie!"

"My dear, dragons are creatures of fire," he said, as though that settled everything.

Sure. I know that. Everybody knows that. Dragons breathe fire. All the fairy tales say so. "OK. What does that have to do with anything?"

"Well, coming into contact with the Atlantean amulet woke up your affinity with darkness, but it woke other things up too. I think perhaps coming into contact with the dragon scale may have, I don't know, activated your fire affinity."

"Are you talking," I hissed, "about kissing fire? Like in the book?" Eddie's book is like nothing I've ever seen before. It is, in a strange way, sentient. It seems to sense what we want to know about all things supernatural and, very often, will show us what we need.

"I believe so, yes."

"Oh, sweet lords above. Jack is going to freak out."

"Why would he do that?" Eddie asked.

"Because I sort of left Portland without telling him and without the amulet, and now I've got a stupid new superpower and he's not here to help." I sucked in a deep breath. I was going to hyperventilate at this rate. "There's something else, Eddie." I told him about my dream, leaving nothing out. He was quiet for a moment. His silence made me nervous. "So?"

"Well, remember how I told you about the elemental mages?"

Of course I remembered. How could I forget? The elemental mages had been descendants of the ancient Atlanteans, able to channel the elements.

"It sounds like you were dreaming about a fire mage."

"A fire mage? Oh, goody." Fina would have been the fire mage, which would have left Iah as...what? I had no idea what the moon represented.

"Well, it would make sense. It seems you are starting to channel fire, so perhaps the dreams are trying to tell you something."

"What about the dragon calling her a fire bringer?"

I heard the sound of pages turning.

"Is that the book, Eddie?" I would never admit it to anyone, but Eddie's sentient book kind of freaks me out despite the fact that it pretty much has an answer for everything.

"Naturally. Let me see...Ah, yes, here it is." He cleared his throat. "Nothing here about a fire bringer, but as I told you before, the elemental mages chose a particular element to worship and learned to channel that element as a form of power. A very few were so good at it, so powerful, they went mad and had to be killed. Perhaps that's what you were seeing."

I shook my head, then realized Eddie couldn't see me. Oh, the joys of jet lag. "No, I don't think so. I mean, not exactly. These people were very young, and I got the feeling that they hadn't chosen the elements so much as been born with them. The woman kept thinking of the man as, I don't know, a moon child, for lack of a better term. He was the first male on record to be born with an affinity for the moon. They didn't even have a male name for him. Don't know what that was about."

"What were their names?"

"He called her Fina. His name was Iah."

"Ah, yes. Fina, short for Sarafina. She was a fire goddess. Iah was a moon god, thousands of years older. They must have been named for the elements they chose."

"Or that chose them," I reminded him.

"It is possible that the truth of the matter has been lost to time," Eddie admitted. "There could have been some who were born already channeling their power."

"It seemed like it. They were too young to have spent the number of years in practice the book indicated. But let me tell you, the woman was freaked. She killed herself, Eddie. She kept saying, or thinking, that she couldn't control the fire. There was such...rage in her, such hunger. To burn. To destroy." That was what really freaked me out. Because I feel the same thing with the darkness. And now I'd started setting things on fire...

Eddie sighed. "It sounds like she was burning out. If she were born with the power, she should have had better control over it, but from what you've described, it seems she didn't. She killed herself to save those she loved."

"In other words, she was about to go critical?"

"Yes, indeed."

As if the darkness weren't hard enough to deal with, I was now channeling a power that might make me blow up and take a city with it. *Oh, shit.* That was not good. Did that mean I was going to be a danger to the people I loved too? That I could go critical like Fina? Destroy my friends? My family?

Oh, gods. What was I going to do?

The only thing I could do was focus on the matter at hand. Get as much information as I could so I could deal with...whatever. I had to push through the terror and do what needed to be done.

"But what about this moon guy? That's not an element."

"Oh, yes, that's an interesting one." Eddie had his lecturer voice on. "The moon is often associated with nature worship. Artemis was both moon goddess and nature goddess, goddess of the hunt. This Iah was most likely able to channel Earth."

"That would make sense. So he was an earth mage, and she was a fire mage who fed herself to a dragon. And that's another thing. She seemed to be friends with the dragon, despite the fact that it killed her. Not exactly the same picture of dragons Alister painted."

"Hmm, interesting, let's see." More page flipping. "Ah, yes. It appears that elemental mages often had affinity with supernatural creatures of their element. Dragons are of fire; therefore, it would make sense for a fire mage to befriend a dragon. Odd choice for friendship, but there you go."

"So the dragon burned her out of friendship?"

"Yes, of course." He seemed surprised I would doubt it. "The water most likely would not have destroyed her power permanently. Dampened it maybe, but not destroyed it. Even after death, her body would have given into the fire—explosions, fireballs, that sort of thing. The water would have only prevented the destruction of those on land. You've heard the saying 'fight fire with fire.'"

Fantastic. So if I had these powers, I was going to wind up eaten by a dragon. Then a thought occurred.

"Eddie, I have an affinity with vampires. They're not my friends, but…" I couldn't finish the thought.

"You're wondering whether that affinity has something to do with the darkness?"

"Yes." My voice was small. I didn't like how weak and helpless all this elemental stuff made me feel.

"It's possible, of course, but not necessarily so. After all, you are a hunter. Hunters often have an affinity of some nature with their prey. That's what makes them good at their jobs." His voice was hearty and cheering. It made me smile. Eddie always tries to make me feel better, no matter how bad the news. He is like a wonderful, crazy uncle with bad fashion sense. I decided then and there I was going to bring him back something breathtakingly tacky to wear. Like Union Jack boxer shorts. He'd love them.

"Eddie, what do I do?"

"I don't know." He sounded worried, and that didn't make me feel any better. "For now, just try to control it like you do the darkness."

Oh, yeah, because that is so easy.

"In the meantime," he continued, "I'll do some more research. And, Morgan, you will be careful, won't you?"

"Of course, Eddie. When am I not?"

It was probably a good thing he didn't answer that.

"I really think you ought to talk to Jack, my dear." Eddie's voice grew quieter. "If anyone would know how to help you, it would be him. He hasn't seen nine hundred years for nothing."

By "help" I knew he really meant "save." I must have been in a hell of a lot more trouble than I'd realized. I felt like throwing up. And then maybe locking myself in my room and bawling my eyes out. Eddie had no idea what had happened between Jack and me and that there was no way I could call Jack for help.

"Thanks, Eddie. I knew I could count on you."

"Always, my dear." I heard the sadness in his voice under the false bravado. Right then, I felt more scared and alone than I'd ever been. Even on the night I died.

∽

I didn't sleep much the rest of the night. The idea of having another nightmare combined with the very real possibility that this stupid fire thing could kill me was enough to keep anyone awake. Naturally, Kabita noticed the next morning.

"You look like crap," she said over the rim of her coffee mug.

"Gee, thanks. If you don't stop with the flattery, I might get a big head." I slapped some butter on a croissant and took a bite.

"Too late."

I flipped her off and took another bite of croissant. My stomach wasn't feeling pleased this morning. I knew I'd be hungry in an hour, but bread was the only thing that didn't make me feel like hurling.

"Didn't sleep well?" Her voice held a bit more sympathy.

"Not so much, no. I had another dream." I'd told Kabita about the other dreams. The ones about the high priest of Atlantis, the Templar Knight, and the last princess of Atlantis. She didn't take them quite as seriously as I did, but then, she wasn't the one having them. Nor was she the one channeling weird mystical energies. Or whatever. "You talked to Eddie?"

"Yeah, of course. He was quite helpful." I paused. "He wants me to talk to Jack."

She raised a brow. "Then why don't you? I know stuff happened between you, but…"

I hadn't told her everything that had gone on between Jack and me—just that it was over. I hadn't been able to talk about it at the time, and then there'd been her cousin's murder.

"I can't call him." I couldn't quite help the sadness that crept into my voice. "We had amazing chemistry. I really thought we were going somewhere, and then this stupid Atlantean royal bloodline thing happens and he freaks out and heads for the hills."

"You want me to show him my ninja junk punch skills?"

I laughed at that. "Thanks, but no. I'm trying to make him see sense, not scare the daylights out of him. Though he was a Templar Knight, so I doubt he'd be all that scared."

"He should be." Her face was calm, her voice expressionless. She kind of scared *me* when she did that.

"Well, I'll keep it in mind, should my powers of persuasion not work." Which, so far, they hadn't. I might need her NJP skills, after all.

"Good." She set down her cup. "What's on the agenda for today?"

"Sandra Fuentes invited me to her shop in Soho, so I thought I'd head over there. I've a feeling that woman knows a lot more than she's saying. It would be good to have a longer chat with her." I tossed the remainder of my croissant onto my plate. My appetite just wasn't there.

Kabita nodded. "Good idea. She's definitely got more up her sleeve than she's showing, and she appeared to like you. Goddess knows why."

I chucked the croissant at her. "How about you?"

"I was thinking of heading over to Julia's place. See if there's anything useful MI8 missed. I've got a meeting with an old client first, though, so I'll head over after lunch."

"Why don't I go with you? We can meet up after you do your meeting thing and my visit with Sandra." I really didn't want her going to her cousin's apartment alone. She was putting on a brave face, but I knew her well enough to know that the whole investigation into her cousin's death, along with having to deal with her dad, was really hard for her. It would be hard for anyone.

She looked relieved. "Yeah, that sounds good. I'll text you her address, and we'll meet there at two."

I nodded and headed for the lobby. I still felt shaky and disoriented from the dream. "Pull yourself together, Morgan," I muttered under my breath. "This is no time to fall apart."

I wasn't sure the pep talk worked, but as I stepped out into the sun, I felt a little better. I might not know yet what to do about my fabulous new superpowers, but at least I was doing something for Julia. Maybe in finding her answers, I'd find some of my own.

Chapter Ten

Sometimes, when you haven't lived in a place for a long time, you forget the little things that annoyed you. Hordes of tourists are one of those things.

As I dodged yet another couple stopped dead in the middle of the pavement to gawk at something or other, I tried to rein in my temper. Honestly, some people don't have the brains the gods gave a turnip.

It was a gorgeous sunny day, and Carnaby Street was packed. It shouldn't have surprised me. Carnaby is such a cute little street, crammed with beautiful little shops filled with all kinds of treasures. Then I saw something that stopped me in my tracks.

Just ahead of me, headed my way, were two men. They were tall and well built, but not overly muscular. They were holding hands, but that was nothing unusual. Soho is known as the gay mecca of London, so two men holding hands is pretty much par for the course. The thing that stopped me was their faces.

Their almost-too-handsome faces kept shifting. One minute they wore one face, and the next time you looked they each had a different one, their faces molding and changing from one incarnation to the next.

No one else seemed to see it, but I did. They were sidhe.

My first run-in with the sidhe had been at the supernatural nightclub Fringe back when I'd first been hunting Jack. It had only been a brief encounter, but you never forget an encounter with the sidhe.

The two men drew closer, and as they passed me, they nodded at me in unison. My heart froze, then started pounding double time. They'd noticed me. For the second time in a matter of months, the sidhe had not only noticed me, they'd acknowledged my presence with something almost like respect. I shuddered at the thought. I had no idea why the sidhe were suddenly taking such a keen interest in me, and I didn't like it.

It is never a good thing to come to the attention of the sidhe. They have a way of making life very difficult. Even if they like you. Though they are more likely to dislike you, and then you are in deep shit.

The sidhe disappeared around a corner. Suddenly, I could breathe easier.

I darted left up Ganton Street and finally found Sandra's shop tucked in between a men's tailor and a shoe shop. Honestly, you couldn't miss it. The trim around the front window was painted a bright golden yellow, while the door was a hot, fiery orange. Orange letters picked out in gold across the window proclaimed THE DRAGON'S DEN.

The best thing about the shop had to be the enormous papier-mâché dragon taking up the entire front window. It was painted fire-engine red, with gold-and-orange accents and yellow jewels for eyes. It was incredibly impressive, and I wondered whether this was another result of Sandra's own particular brand of magic or if she'd actually made it by hand.

A little bell above the door tinkled as I entered the store, reminding me of Eddie's shop back in Portland. I suffered a tiny pang of homesickness. How could a person be homesick for two different places?

"Morgan Bailey! Welcome to my shop. I'm so thrilled you've come." Sandra came bustling out from behind the counter, wrapping me in a perfume-scented hug. She might not look much like her sister, but she is just as effusive and has the same sense of drama, if her outfit was anything to go by.

Sandra was dressed in a flowing white gown with a scoop neck and long bell sleeves like something out of a tale of Camelot. She must have been wearing a seriously good bra, because her chest was boosted to the sky, showing an enormous amount of cleavage. Gold cords were wrapped around her waist in Grecian style to match her gold sandals, and she was wearing a crimson cloak, of all things.

A multitude of gold bracelets jangled on her arm as she waved to indicate the rows upon rows of dragon paraphernalia. "Isn't it marvelous? I dreamed about a shop like this for such a long time. Then my third husband died and left me quite a lot of money. *Voilà!* The Dragon's Den was born."

It was quite something. I didn't think I'd ever seen so many items to do with dragons in one place in my life. There were dragon statuettes, papier-mâché dragons, dragon paperweights, and paintings of dragons. An entire wall was devoted to shelves of books about dragons. There was even a glass case with a sign that claimed the artifacts inside the case were dragon artifacts, though it mostly looked like a bunch of old bones and bits of leather to me.

"It's great, Sandra. Really amazing."

She beamed at me. "Why, thank you. It really was a labor of love."

"Do you sell many dragons?"

"Oh, much more online than in the shop, of course. But you never know when a person will need a dragon."

"No, I suppose not," I murmured. I wondered what sort of emergency would require a person to hit the streets of London searching out dragon statues. I also wondered vaguely how to broach the subject of her abilities, and whether hers were anything like Cordelia's.

"I suppose," she said, leaning against the counter, "you're wondering how to broach the subject of my magic."

I must have looked startled, because she let out a laugh very much like Cordelia's. "It was written all over your face. You've a very expressive face, Morgan. You show the world everything you're feeling."

Great. And here I'd thought I was good at hiding my emotions.

"Since you mention it, yes, I would like to know more about your ability. How long have you been able to do...what you do?"

"Oh, all my life," she said. "I was still an infant when I turned my rattle dragon shaped. At least that's what my mother told me, though of course I don't remember it. When I was three, I did it again. This time with the milk jug. Now, that I do remember. You can imagine the mess!"

I found her stories difficult to believe. It wasn't that I didn't believe she had such a power—I'd already seen it myself—but that she'd been manifesting it in infancy seemed far-fetched. Abilities such as hers very rarely showed up before puberty, and never with such incredible results. But I kept my face still, trying not to show my doubt. It didn't work. Apparently, I need to work on my impassive face.

"You don't believe me, of course," she said with a smile. "I don't blame you. It's not as though I could prove it. My mother was there, but my mother was a bit unstable, so no one believed her, either."

This was the first I'd heard of Cordy's mother being nuts, but then again, it isn't something you just bring up in conversation generally. And while Cordelia and I have known each other for quite a while, I imagine she doesn't feel comfortable sharing with many people.

"Cordy didn't tell you?"

"Uh, no."

She shrugged. "I'm not sure she understood. We were both very young when Mother died. Still, the fact remains that my ability has always been with me. I did it again when I was four—turned a teaspoon into a figure of a dragon. I remember it clearly. We were at the dinner table, and Father was furious because they were silver spoons. Even worse, his mother was there, and she was not a fan."

"Of magic?"

"That. And my mother. Considered her a bad influence on my father." She laughed again, and it was light and bright like Cordy's. "Trust me, my father needed a bad influence in his life. Anyway," she continued, "here it is all these years later and I'm still turning things into dragons."

"Why?"

She looked a bit confused by that. "What do you mean, why?"

"Why dragons, specifically? I mean, why not monkeys or elephants or mermaids?"

"Oh, yes, it is rather odd, isn't it?" She shrugged. "I don't really know why dragons. They're just in my head. All the time. I suppose you could say I'm obsessed."

I gazed around the shop. Obsessed was a good word for it.

"Of course, my husband thinks I'm a bit bonkers. But what does he know? He's a tech mage, after all. Not exactly normal, if you ask me."

"I thought you said your husband was dead?"

"Oh, that was husband number three, dear. This is husband four. He's quite lovely, number four. Even if he is overly fond of fiddling with his gizmos."

I hoped she meant he was doing his tech mage thing and messing about bonding magic and technology and not…something else. I also wondered vaguely whether Four had a name. Maybe Sandra had gone through so many husbands she'd given up learning their names and started calling them by numbers. The thought made me grin.

"I was hoping you could tell me more about dragons," I said, bringing her back to the subject at hand. "I see you have some dragon artifacts."

"Oh, those are just for the tourists. They're nothing of interest. The real stuff is back here." She motioned me to follow her through a wrought-iron gate into the back room.

It looked pretty much like the one at Majicks and Potions, just a bit less dusty and much more orderly. Several metal shelving units held boxes of goods meant for sale and paperwork meant for filing. A state-of-the-art laptop sat squarely in the middle of a neatly organized desk, and a file cabinet stood sentry by the door.

Sandra beckoned me behind one of the shelving units to a space not visible from the door. There sat a large metal foot locker, locked tight with a padlock. Sandra took a chain from around her neck. The chain held a single key, which she inserted into the lock.

The lid opened with a slight creak. Inside were several parcels and pouches. Sandra pulled one from the chest and laid it on the floor. Carefully, she untied the bindings and unfolded the dark fabric.

Lying against the cloth was a dragon scale nearly twice the size of the one I had, the one that had been found with Julia's body. I couldn't help but gasp at the size of the thing. "Where did you find this?"

"I didn't," she said. "It was a gift."

"A gift? Who gave it to you?"

Sandra smiled. "Why, a dragon, of course."

Chapter Eleven

I wondered whether I looked as shocked as I felt. Probably. "A dragon gave it to you?"

"Yes, of course. Where else would I get a dragon scale? It's not like they're just lying about waiting to be picked up." She began carefully wrapping it back up.

"So the dragons really do exist."

"They do. There aren't as many as there once were, but they're still out there."

"Out where, exactly?"

"Oh, here and there." She fluttered her hand about vaguely. "You could meet a dragon just about any place. You never know." She pulled another parcel from the trunk, unwrapping it slowly.

"Is that a dragon claw?"

"Yes," she said quietly, running a finger over the enormous ivory claw. "It was taken by a hunter after he killed the dragon it came from. He wore it around his neck as a token of his bravery." There was bitterness in her voice now, and anger.

I noticed the hole drilled at the base of the claw. Someone had definitely turned it into jewelry, and from the looks of things, it wasn't recent.

"You took it back."

"It did not belong to him. For a thousand years, his descendants desecrated the memory of that beautiful creature by wearing this claw like a trophy; I simply freed it. When the time is right, I will return it to its rightful place."

"With the dragons?"

She gave me a look. "Yes."

"Sandra, what would you say about this?" I pulled the warm dragon scale from Julia's crime scene from my pocket and handed it to her. The scale gave me a slight zing as it left my hand.

She turned it over, running her fingers across its surface. Her face glowed with wonder. "Where did you find it?"

"I didn't. MI8 found it on a body. A body that had been clawed to death."

"Julia Reynolds."

I nodded.

She shook her head. "No, that cannot be. If a dragon did kill someone—and it's bloody unlikely—it wouldn't leave a scale behind. Not to mention there wouldn't be much left of the person. Someone planted this." The tone of her voice was one of absolute certainty.

The scale was cool when she handed it back, but the moment it touched my skin, it began to warm.

"That's what I figured." Well, that's what I figured now that I knew dragons weren't actually extinct. But I didn't mention that. "There simply wasn't enough damage to Julia's body for the killer to have been a dragon. Unfortunately, MI8 is working off the premise that Julia was killed by a dragon, and they're not listening to reason." I watched her closely as I shared my information about the MI8 investigation, not terribly surprised as a look of horror swept across her face.

"You must stop them, Morgan. You must. They are innocent. The dragons did not do this! They've left us unharmed for centuries. If they wanted to hurt us, they'd have done so long before now. If you don't stop it, there's going to be another hunt." She twisted her hands in her lap. "It will be genocide."

I reached over and took her hands in mine, stilling them. "I don't want that to happen any more than you do."

"You believe me? But you are a hunter." Her tone told me she held hunters in about the same regard as sewer rats.

I smiled at her and gave her hands a squeeze. "Apparently, I'm not your normal run-of-the-mill hunter." I didn't mention that I wasn't 100 percent convinced the dragons hadn't harmed any humans in centuries. It was enough that I was sure they hadn't killed Julia.

She gave me a trembling smile. "So what are you going to do?"

"The only thing I can do. Find out who really did kill Julia." I released her hands and sat back. "Who would have the most to gain from framing a dragon for murder?"

It was rhetorical, but she answered, "Why, a dragon hunter, of course."

I shook my head. "Hunters like me don't even know about dragons, and there hasn't been a true dragon hunter born in over a century."

She held my gaze for a moment as though deciding whether I was trustworthy. Apparently, the decision was in my favor. "That isn't true."

"What do you mean?" Alister had been very clear that dragon hunters no longer existed. They weren't needed.

"A true dragon hunter was born twenty-three years ago right here in London."

I was late getting to Julia's flat, my head still buzzing with the information I'd learned from Sandra. She didn't know where the dragon hunter was now, but she claimed she had friends "in the know" who'd recorded the birth and tracked the hunter until she'd disappeared five years ago. If Sandra was right and dragon hunters still exist, then either Alister was lying or he was sorely misinformed. Either way, it wasn't good. After all, if he had such a blind hatred of witches, he could very well feel the same about other supernatural beings. And if that were true, what lengths would he be willing to go to destroy them? Would he actually be willing to commit genocide?

I shrugged it off and rapped on the door. It swung open to reveal Kabita.

"Don't give me the Look," I said, giving her one of my own as I stepped past her into the hall.

"You're late."

I rolled my eyes at her. "Believe me, it was worth it." I quickly told her what I'd learned from Sandra.

Kabita's jaw tightened. "So my father is probably hiding something. No surprise there. He always did let his own personal bigotry get in the way of doing the right thing."

"Generally how bigotry works."

She ignored me and headed down the hall toward what I assumed was the main living space. I was right. The hall emptied into a large American-style open-plan living area. A kitchen lay to the left, living room to the right, and dining area down the middle. In front of it all was a wall of glass with an unobstructed view of the city.

"Freaking fantastic," I breathed. "I had no idea MI8 paid this well."

"They don't. Not to peons like Julia. Her grandfather Reynolds came from money. Left her a load when he died." Kabita nodded to the right. "I've cleared the living room. Nothing exciting there. I'll check out the bedroom; you get the kitchen."

"Roger that." I was sure MI8 had already checked the place out pretty thoroughly, but no matter how good an investigative team, things get missed. Not to mention there is nothing quite like seeing a place for yourself.

The kitchen was large by London standards, with all the accoutrements of a modern kitchen, such as a garbage disposal and a dishwasher. Luxuries I hadn't been able to afford back when I lived there. I could now.

I rummaged through the freezer. Classic hiding place of the unimaginative. Nothing. I guess Julia either had an imagination or MI8 had already found whatever she'd hidden. The fridge, oven, and cupboards also revealed nothing. I even went through all the bottles of cleaning products under the sink. Then a thought struck me.

It isn't a particularly unique hiding place, but not everyone thinks of it first thing. I opened one of the cupboards and pulled down a large plastic container filled with flour. I'd seen this in a movie once. I peeled off the lid and stuck my hand into the powdery stuff, swishing it around. Nothing.

I pulled down another container. A cookie jar this time. I felt around until my fingers snagged a plastic bag. I yanked it out of the cookies, spilling crumbs everywhere.

Inside the large sealed bag was a leather-bound journal not much bigger than a deck of cards, each page covered in neat little letters. As I flipped through, a photo fell out onto the floor. I scooped it up. It was a picture of Julia with a big smile stretching across her face. Next to her stood a tall man, one arm wrapped around her shoulders and such a look of adoration on his face it made my heart ache.

It was Julia's colleague from the funeral.

"Kabita! I found Julia's journal."

She hurried out from the bedroom. "Good work." She peered at the pages. "It's all a bunch of gibberish. She must have written it in code."

"That would make sense. She was obviously worried about it being discovered. She hid the thing in a cookie jar. She also hid this." I held out the photo.

"He worked with Julia. I think his name is Landry. Something like that."

I nodded. "I had a feeling he had a thing for Julia. Do you think it was mutual?"

"Looks that way."

"That's just sad." I sighed and tucked the picture back between the pages of the journal. "Do you know how to crack the code?"

She shook her head. "My brother Adam's good with codes, though. I'll let him give it a try. Maybe he can do something with it."

"Here's hoping. I have a feeling there's something important in there."

"I agree." She led the way toward the front door. "I think that's all we're going to find here. Nothing in the bedroom or bathroom, and MI8 already has her computer. I could use a drink. You?"

"Sure, why not. I saw a pub just up the road."

We headed up the street in companionable silence. We've known each other long enough that we don't always need words. I could tell something was eating at Kabita, but I figured she'd share it when the time was right.

It was early yet and the pub was mostly empty, so we had our choice of tables. I sank down at one near the back. I've never been a fan of beer, and wine makes me sleepy. I've found cider to be a nice alternative, so I ordered a pint of pear cider and took a long sip when it came. "Boy, I needed that. This has been a crazy couple of days." It was nice to relax in the dark coziness of the pub.

Kabita smiled and sipped at her wine, but her face was strained.

I frowned. "OK, what is it?"

She sighed. "I'm worried about you, Morgan."

I blinked. "Worried about me? Why?"

"This whole dragon thing. I know you think the dragons are innocent, but I'm not so sure. Dad obviously thinks they're involved."

"Right. And your father is the pinnacle of fairness and honesty." My voice dripped with sarcasm.

Her jaw tightened. It made me feel bad. Just a little. It was obvious her father told the truth only when it suited him. He hated everything his daughter was, for crying out loud. Yet here she was getting all upset at my calling a spade a spade. Then again, I supposed I'd be protective of my family too.

"I'm sorry, Kabita, but come on. Alister hasn't been entirely forthcoming. About anything. It's pretty clear he's been keeping things from us. He could have even sent that blonde woman to spy on us. I'd be willing to bet he's known all along that dragon hunters are still around. He's the head of MI8, for goodness' sake."

"It isn't just the dragons, Morgan. You're obsessed."

"With what?" My temper was rapidly fraying.

"With the vampire who killed you," she said. I started to speak, but she held up her hand. "I know, I know. You have every right to be a little obsessed with hunting that monster, but I'm still worried. Hunting down your own murderer is a little…"

"Freaky?" I suggested.

"That's certainly one way of putting it," said someone from behind me.

My stomach dropped. I knew that voice. It was a little more gravelly than I'd remembered, but no less sexy. I turned slowly in my seat. "What the hell are you doing here?" I couldn't help the tiny twinge of hope that he'd changed his mind.

Jack stood behind me. His beautifully sculpted face was stoic, but his sea-blue eyes burned with fire. He was angry. Really angry. "I told you. I can find you anywhere."

"That's a little stalkerish." I couldn't help the anger that crept into my voice. He didn't want to be with me, but it was OK to follow me across the globe?

"You left Portland without saying good-bye. You didn't take the amulet with you. And now you're chasing all over the city of London after a vampire you think killed you three years ago."

"I don't think. I *know* he's the one that killed me. I'll never forget the smell of him." My lip curled at the memory. It might sound crazy, but I knew that vamp was following me. I knew it in my very bones.

"Maybe so, but it's not just the vampire; it's the dragons too." I hadn't noticed the second man standing a little behind Jack until he spoke.

"Trevor Daly. Fancy meeting you here. Is there some reason you think what I do is your business?"

He sat down at the table and leaned toward me, his brown eyes flashing with anger. "You work for Kabita, and Kabita works for me; therefore, everything you do is my business."

"Bullshit. I'm on my own time." I took a deep gulp of cider. "What I do on my own time is my business. What the hell are you doing here, anyway?"

"I ran into Jack on the plane over and we got to talking. Realized we were after the same thing, finding you two. We decided to…join forces, as it were."

"Lovely." My voice was dry as dust. That was all I needed. Jack and Trevor on the same team.

"And you're not on your own time anymore. This is now an official joint investigation." The look Trevor gave me was just a little too smug for my liking.

"Excuse me? Don't you think you're a little out of your jurisdiction?"

"MI8 invited him." Kabita's voice was quiet, calm. She probably knew I was about to turn into Vesuvius.

"MI8? Why?" I couldn't imagine Alister would enjoy having the Americans on his turf. They had no beef with the dragons and might not accept everything he said blindly.

"They had no choice. I'm the American dragon liaison." Yep. Trevor's smile was definitely too smug.

I snorted. "American dragon liaison? Are you kidding me?"

He shrugged. "Granted, I haven't had anything to do until now, but the US government has always had an official liaison. Just in case."

I blew out a deep breath. "Well, I guess 'just in case' finally happened. I suppose you want to blow the dragons to bits too. Never mind what the evidence says."

"No, Morgan." Trevor shook his head. He placed his hand over mine, his mocha skin rich against the pale alabaster of my own. He has broad, strong hands. Something about their shape reminded me of my father's hands in the picture of him I carried with me in my wallet wherever I went.

I jerked my hand away. "Isn't that what all you bureaucratic types like to do? Shoot first, ask questions later?"

He laughed at that. "I think you've got me mixed up with the military." He leaned forward again, eyes intense. "I promise you, Morgan, I will do this right. I will not rest until I find the truth. I will make my decision based on facts, not fear or ignorance."

I believed him. Somehow, I believed him.

"Morgan," Jack spoke again, "we need to talk." He held out his hand.

I hesitated. There was so much that was screwed up between us, and I couldn't help that, deep down, I felt hurt. Rejected. Still, he wanted to talk—that was something.

I reluctantly placed my hand in his, and the electricity went zinging up and down my spine. Just like always. The chemistry between us hadn't changed, no matter how Jack tried to hide it. Bloody stubborn man.

I followed him out of the pub while Kabita and Trevor remained, chatting in low voices. I imagined they were discussing the case and our role in it. I hoped I wasn't being an idiot by trusting Trevor Daly. If he screwed me over, there'd be hell to pay.

Chapter Twelve

Why didn't you tell me you were leaving?" Jack's voice was quiet, calm, as we stepped outside the pub and moved down the sidewalk, but I could hear something else simmering underneath. I wasn't sure whether it was hurt or anger. Maybe a little of both. Not that I cared much. He'd hurt me plenty.

"There wasn't time." I dodged a tourist snapping a picture of some random building. Honestly, sometimes I really wish I had a cattle prod.

Jack gave me a look that said he didn't buy my excuse.

"Fine." I heaved a sigh. "I knew you'd freak out, and I didn't want to deal with it."

"Freak out?" His voice was mild, but he didn't fool me.

"You know what I mean. You'd give me some lecture on how you couldn't protect me if I went traipsing off into the wilds of London, yada yada. I can protect myself, you know. I'm a hunter, for crying out loud."

He smiled at that. "You know me well."

"Not as well as I'd like to." *Crap. Did I say that out loud?*

"Morgan." It was his turn to sigh.

"I'm sorry, Jack." I stopped in the middle of the pavement just like a bloody tourist and propped my fists on my hips. "I just don't get it. One minute you're on me like white on rice, and the next I'm untouchable. All because of a piece of jewelry. You really know how to make a girl feel good."

His features were tight, every inch of him strung taut with frustration. "I've told you Morgan. It's my duty—"

"Fuck your duty."

The shock on his face was priceless.

"You've given, what, nine hundred years of your life to duty? To protecting the amulet. To some dream of a royal bloodline and saving Atlantis and whatever else comes with the territory. Hell, I don't even know what it is you think you're going to do with that thing. I think it's time you do something for yourself for a change."

For us.

"You should at least have brought the amulet with you," he said, completely ignoring the point.

"You're trying to change the subject, Jack. It isn't going to work." I turned on my heel and marched down South Audley Street, fury strumming through me. Gods, the man can piss me off like nobody else.

I stormed across the street, barely giving the traffic any attention. Ahead was Grosvenor Square, with its small grassy part on the right and the squat, ugly building housing the American embassy on the left. It is a lovely part of central London despite the eyesore.

The guards in front of the embassy gave me leery looks, as though they half expected me to go ballistic at any minute. The thought almost made me laugh. Almost. I kept walking.

Jack finally caught up to me. "I am not going to discuss this with you, Morgan," he said, jaw clenched.

"Hey, you were the one who wanted to talk."

"Not about this. You know what I must do. I will not shirk my duty."

I rolled my eyes. "Good lord. You'd think we were still in the Dark Ages. Fine, you don't want to talk about it, I'll give you a pass. For now. But we *will* talk about it. Soon." Truth was, I was feeling a little overly emotional and not entirely ready to talk about it myself.

He said nothing to that. I shrugged. A girl can only do so much. "As for the amulet, it doesn't go with my wardrobe."

"Morgan Bailey." His voice was practically a growl.

"Listen, I am not walking around with some big clunky thing on my neck—especially some big clunky thing that turns me into a supernatural superconductor. I have enough problems in my life as it is. Anyway, how'd you find me?"

"I figured Eddie would know what was going on with you, so I gave him a call. He told me where you were."

My breath came out in a hiss. "I told Eddie not to tell you." I glared at another tourist, and she scrambled out of the way like I'd pointed a gun at her. Maybe I didn't need a cattle prod after all.

"Eddie decided that your setting a door on fire was something I needed to know about." He led me across the road to Hyde Park and down one of the tree-lined paths. It was nearly dark, but there were still plenty of people about.

"I would have told you."

"When?"

I shrugged. "Eventually."

"Morgan." His voice was filled with frustration. "This is not something to mess with. It's dangerous. You could die." His voice seemed to catch a little on that last part. "You could lose control and..."

And go critical. Like in my dream. "I know that. Don't you think I know that? But what can I do? This amulet of yours has decided it wants to download all these stupid abilities into me, and there's nothing I can do to stop it." Which was part of the reason I didn't want to wear the damn thing. I was hoping to postpone the inevitable.

"Morgan..."

"Listen, I don't want to talk about it right now." My turn to be uncooperative. "Unless you have something useful to tell me, like what this new ability or whatever is or how to get rid of it?"

Silence.

"Fine. I'm done. When you decide you're ready to talk about us, then I'll talk about this. Maybe."

He shoved his hands in his jeans pockets and shook his head, frustration in every line of his body. I knew I was driving him insane, and part of me was glad. After all, he'd been driving me crazy lately with his stupid duty and honor stuff.

Uncomfortable moments passed with Jack saying nothing and me unsure of what to say. There was so much unresolved between us, but for once, I had no idea where to start. I wasn't sure I even wanted to.

I decided it was time for a subject change. I figured if anybody would know anything about dragons and Sandra's abilities, it would be Jack. I bet you meet a lot of interesting people in nine hundred years.

"I met Cordelia's twin sister. She seems to know an awful lot about dragons." I gave him a quick rundown on my meetings with Sandra and what she'd told me about dragon hunters. "She has this amazing ability to turn objects like rocks or spoons or whatever into miniature dragons. I've never seen anything like it."

"Can she turn objects into anything other than dragons?" he asked.

"No. Just dragons."

"Interesting. She may be a dragon child."

I stopped dead in the middle of the footpath. "A what?"

"They're rare. I've only met one before, and that was nearly five hundred years ago. You know how you have an affinity with vampires?"

"Uh, yeah. If by affinity you mean I can track and kill them better than normal people."

"Dragon children are human children born with an affinity with dragons. Unlike hunters, they are born of peace, not violence. In ancient times, before they disappeared from history, the dragons often used dragon children as intermediaries with humans. They helped settle disputes, calm troubles between the species, even negotiate settlements."

I frowned at the thought of being born of violence. In my case, it had been more like being reborn in violence. Then another thought struck me. "I thought the dragons just wanted to eat us."

He laughed, but it wasn't an amused laugh. "I bet Alister Jones told you that."

"Yeah. You know him?"

"We've met." His tone didn't invite further questioning. It was obvious there was history there, but I wasn't inclined to ask, seeing as how I wasn't exactly sharing my own secrets.

"You think Sandra Fuentes is one of these dragon children?" I asked.

"Yes, I do. It would explain the way her magic manifests, the reason she can manipulate objects, but only in a very specific way."

"It would also explain her rather passionate defense of the dragons. She doesn't think they murdered Julia any more than I do." I continued down the path, Jack following suit. I quickly explained the murder and the evidence left behind.

"I believe she is correct. A dragon child may be a soul of peace, but she would never lie to protect the guilty. It would not be in her nature."

"You seem very sure of that," I said.

"As I said, I've met a dragon child before." Again, his tone implied he wasn't interested in talking about it. I imagine that, after nine hundred years, he holds a lot of secrets, and Jack isn't the type of man to give up his secrets easily. A fact that frustrates—and fascinates—me to no end.

"So Alister lied about the dragons. About them killing everyone."

"Let's just say that it's in Alister's best interest to blur the lines of truth."

Interesting. I wondered how exactly Jack knew so much about Alister. I nodded. "Yeah, I get that about him. Sort of like the whole thing with him and his ancestors and witches."

"Yes, something like that."

"OK." I stopped again, this time at a fork in the path. "I'm heading back to my hotel. I need time to think."

"Morgan—" he started, but I cut him off.

"Hyde Park is perfectly safe." He looked doubtful, so I reached out and gave his shoulder a little squeeze. "Stop worrying, Jack. I'll be fine."

After a moment, he nodded reluctantly. "I'll head back to the pub. I'll see you tomorrow?" There was just a hint of something in his voice that gave me hope. Maybe he wasn't quite the immovable rock he seemed.

"Fine." I stood on tiptoe and kissed his cheek, inhaling the scent of him. It felt like ages since I'd touched him, tasted him—though in truth, it had only been just over a week.

Before I could draw back, Jack turned his head and caught my lips with his. Or maybe it wasn't Jack. Maybe it was me. In any case, the next thing I knew our arms were wrapped around each other and we were kissing each other like we might never see each other again.

"Morgan." Jack pulled away a little, his long, lean body still pressed up against mine.

Gods, what I would love to do to that body.

Jack must have read something of what I was thinking, because his ocean-colored eyes grew dark and hooded, and his tongue darted out to flick against his lips. I bit back a groan.

"I've missed you, Morgan."

I froze in place for half a second, eyes closed, before slowly blowing out a breath. I admit I'd been conflicted—was still conflicted—about what had happened between us, and then his reaction. The whole "I'm a holy warrior with a sacred duty so I can't be with you" shit. It so didn't go down with me. Especially since it was rather like closing the barn door behind the horse.

Still, his words were exactly what I'd longed to hear. I felt a little thrill of hope.

"Your choice, Jack. You're the one who's so hell-bent on placing your duty above anything we could have together."

"Maybe I've changed my mind." His voice was so low I wasn't sure I'd heard him.

"Excuse me?"

"You heard me. Screw duty. You're right. It's been more than nine hundred years, and for the first time ever, I've found someone who matters more than duty. It's time for a change." He reached out and pulled me to him. I felt naked and more than a little vulnerable.

"Jack…" I wanted to believe him. I did. But fool me once and all that.

"Shh." He placed his finger over my lips. "Just let me look at you." His eyes traveled my body, hunger in his gaze. He sucked in a breath. "You are a wonder, Morgan Bailey."

It wasn't the first time he'd told me that. I felt my own body grow languid and full, heat pooling between my thighs. Whatever had gone on between us, I wanted him. I always wanted him.

Somehow we made it back to the hotel. My hands fumbled nervously with the lock, and I dropped the key card twice before Jack took it from me.

Inside my room, I held out my hand, and he came, bent his head, and kissed me. His tongue swirled through my mouth, tasting of spice and musk and man. Of Jack.

He groaned as I slid my hand along his chest, down over his stomach, until it rested over the thick erection straining at his jeans. I smiled against his mouth. In that moment, I knew we had a chance. The thought made me incredibly happy.

I reached up and began unbuttoning his shirt, slowly revealing inch after inch of beautifully bronzed skin. On each little inch, I laid a kiss.

Jack's hands slid around to my ass, molding, squeezing, shaping. I grew more and more aroused, until I had no more patience and ripped the rest of his shirt off. His jeans came next, and I paused just long enough to take in the beauty of his body.

The first time we'd been together, I hadn't had the chance to notice his scars. There are plenty. Ancient slash marks across ribs, stomach, and arms. Battle scars of a Templar Knight.

I traced one that cut across his left pectoral, right above his heart. I pressed my mouth to it, feeling the strong beat of his heart beneath.

"Enough," he groaned. "You are driving me to madness."

"Oh, goody," I whispered, my voice huskier than usual, "I always wanted to do that."

With a laugh, he grabbed me and threw me back on the bed, following me down. Legs and arms and mouths tangled together. Hot, so hot I was burning alive.

I traced the line of his back until I found his ass and did some squeezing of my own. "I want you, Jack. Now."

I grabbed a condom from the bedside table. Within seconds, I felt him at my entrance, and then he was inside me, all that hot, hard length of him. My body tightened around him as I arched off the bed. Gods, it felt good.

He began to move inside me, every stroke driving me mad, pushing me closer and closer to the edge until he pushed me up and over. I came with his name on my lips and heat in my eyes.

"Welcome, Hunter."

I blinked. The voice was so deep it rumbled in my chest like stereo bass turned up too loud. Problem was, I couldn't find a person to go with the voice.

I glanced about and felt my heart lodge itself in my throat. I was standing on top of a rock wall with a sheer drop hundreds of feet to the valley below. Fortunately, the wall was wide enough I could take a step back from the edge.

Cold wind tugged at my clothes and hair, just a hint of snow in its breath. The sun struggled weakly against clouds heavy with impending rain. Below, the valley stretched for miles until it became a forest thick with trees. Not the enormous evergreens of home, but the shorter aspens and birch of Northern England and Scotland. They were naked now, the trees, but would be beautiful in the spring, furred with pale-green leaf buds.

To my right was a giant tree, bare of leaves, but I knew it to be an oak. It grew right up through the middle of the ancient stone wall.

"Wait a minute." My voice filled with wonder. "This is Hadrian's Wall."

"Correct, Hunter. This wall has been standing for nearly two thousand years and will most likely stand for two thousand yet. You stand on history."

He wasn't kidding, but I still couldn't spot the owner of the voice. "Yes, it's very cool. But why am I here?"

"Because, Hunter, we brought you here. There are things that need to be said. Truths that need to be told. Lies that need undoing."

"OK." I turned around, still trying to find the speaker. No luck. The wind blew strands of violet-red hair across my eyes. I impatiently brushed them out of the way before turning back to the view of the valley. Even with winter approaching, it was beautiful, green and lush, with tiny white sheep dotting the landscape. "You want to talk? Let's talk. But first, I want to see you. It's kind of hard to hold a conversation with air."

A chuckle so deep it made the wall itself vibrate. "Ever the hunter. Always you want evidence. Never can you take a thing on faith."

"Faith? What does this have to do with faith?"

"Everything. Nothing."

I growled under my breath. "Listen, mister, whoever you are, I don't like riddles. I want to know who you are and what I'm doing here."

"You are here because I bade you to come here. You need to know the truth."

"And what is the truth?" My voice was just this side of a snarl.

"The truth"—the voice moved closer, though I still couldn't see anyone, just a windswept vista from the top of the wall, hot breath puffing against my ear—*"the truth is that we did not do this thing of which we are accused. We would never do this thing, despite the lies told about our kind. This you must know, and this you must prove."*

"I don't know what you're talking about." Confusion sent my mind into turmoil. What "thing" was he talking about? What had he been accused of, and who had accused him? And while we were at it, who the heck was "we"?

"This." The word was a sibilant hiss, strung out on a breath. As the word ended, a picture appeared before me. A beautiful young woman, blonde hair spread across a pillow. Eyes closed as though in peaceful sleep.

Yet her too-white body lay in a pool of crimson blood. Skin slashed from breast to pubic bone, organs exposed, spilling from the wound. The stench of blood and death assaulted me. I gagged and placed a shaking hand across my mouth. I'd seen worse, smelled worse, but I hadn't had time to brace myself. Besides which, I knew the face that lay on that pillow.

"What is this?" I demanded.

"You know."

"Julia."

"Yes." *The sibilance was back in the rumbling voice, a wisp of smoke chasing away the smell of death.*

"Who are you?" *The vision of Julia shimmered and shifted until before me stood a horror of another kind.*

"I am Dragon."

∽

I came awake with a start, the scent of blood and smoke still lingering in my nose. The dream had been as real as the others, but one thing was different. While the dragon theme of the dream had reminded me of the one I'd had about Fina, in this dream, I'd been myself. Not a knight or a priest. Not a mage or a princess. Just me.

It was still dark out, but I turned to find Jack already awake and pulling on his jeans. I frowned. "What are you doing?"

"I'm leaving." His voice was grim.

My heart stuttered to a halt. "Excuse me?"

White lines bracketed his mouth, and he sank down on the bed, burying his face in his hands. "You heard me. This was a mistake. We should never have done this." With a shake of his head, he stood up and pulled his shirt on, every line of his body weary.

Anger burned through me, closely followed by pain. "Guilt. You feel guilty again, don't you?"

He said nothing, which infuriated me even more.

And worse, it hurt. In a way that after Alex—my ex-fiancé who'd ripped out my heart and stomped all over it, the reason I had moved to London in the first place—I'd sworn nothing would ever hurt me again.

"This is bullshit, Jack." I hauled ass out of bed. I didn't even care that I was buck naked. "You can't do this to me again. You can't just come in here, give me some sweet talk and a fuck, and then go back to your high-and-mighty duty like nothing happened."

"I'm sorry, Morgan. This is the way it has to be. I shouldn't have come." His eyes were wells of agony, but frankly, I didn't give a shit. I was tired of him treating me like a booty call and then pulling the duty-and-honor card afterward.

The pain, the humiliation, it was too much. My throat burned with unshed tears. But there was no way in hell I was letting him see me cry.

I yanked the sheet off the bed and wrapped myself in it, then stormed to the door and flung it open. "Get out."

"Morgan…"

My voice was quiet. "Get. Out."

There was sadness in every line of him, but I felt no pity. Only fury. There was more beneath it, but I didn't dare look. Anger I could deal with, but heartbreak, not so much. I was tired of being thrown away whenever I was inconvenient. If Jack wanted to have issues with our being together, fine. But I was through playing the game.

He hesitated in the doorway. "I'm sorry, Morgan, I—"

"I don't give a crap. I'm done." And I slammed the door in his face. This time I meant it. The pain nearly doubled me over, but there was no way I was going after him. No way I was begging for something I knew he'd never give. I didn't care if he was the guardian of Atlantis or the freaking Tooth Fairy, I was done with Jackson Keel.

တ

I stormed out of the hotel, leaving a fluttering Francois in my wake. It was just past midnight. Earlier than I'd thought.

I hit the park with fury still thrumming through my body. And pain. So much pain I wasn't sure if I wanted to cry or scream or puke. Maybe all three.

My phone chimed, indicating a text message. It was from Kabita.

Ben Landry. Julia's coworker. Meeting tomorrow 10am. Breakfast at 9.

I sent her a text back: *OK. C U at breakfast.* Kabita never used text-speak, and she hated it when I did. Which was why I did it, naturally.

I needed to distract myself from the dull ache that seemed to have taken up residence somewhere in the vicinity of my heart, so I focused my attention on the case. Just exactly what had Ben and Julia's relationship been? Had he told her he loved her? Had she loved him back? I wasn't sure which was worse—losing the person you love or having them there in front of you but totally unreachable. At the moment, it definitely felt like the latter.

It was then that I caught the scent. That same scent that had been taunting me for days, but this time that tingling in the back of my skull came with it.

My vampire was close—really close. I took off at a dead run, following the scent trail that grew stronger with every footstep.

And then what felt like a Mack truck hit me in the side and sent me tumbling across the grass until I landed in a breathless heap. I staggered to my feet, the stench of vampire drowning out everything else. I still couldn't see anything. This time, though, I could smell the reek of a second vamp underneath the original scent trail. Something hinky was definitely going on.

The shadows shifted as I scanned the park. I could barely make out the dim shape of what had to be the vampire who'd just hit me.

I slipped out my knife. I was going to have to get in close without getting myself killed. I didn't have my larger weapons with me, and I was loath to use the darkness. I was afraid that, one of these days, I wouldn't come back from it.

I braced myself as the vamp stepped closer and a shaft of moonlight lit his face. It was not what I expected to see. "You're not the one. You didn't kill me."

"Maybe not," he snarled, putrid breath hitting me full in the face. "But I'm going to kill you now."

He lunged at me, grabbing me around the throat and throwing me to the ground. There was no way I could stab him through the chest in this position, so I went for the kidneys. Contrary to popular belief, you don't need to stab a vamp through the heart. Technically, massive blood loss can do it, though it usually isn't fast enough.

The knife went through his back, slicing tissue and muscle and sliding into organs, the silver tip burning him like acid. Cold blood spilled over my hand. The vamp screamed loud enough to make my ears ring.

I ripped the knife back out, causing as much damage as I could on the way. Then, as the vamp reared back, I sliced backward across his throat. More blood cascaded from the wound, drenching me. I turned my face to avoid getting the vile stuff in my mouth.

I twisted, heaving the dying vamp off me. I knelt on him, the tip of the blade over his heart. "Who sent you?" I hissed at him.

Underneath his own scent, I could still smell the scent of the vampire who'd killed me. His jacket looked lumpy, so I fished around and pulled out a dirty old T-shirt. It stank of vampire. Not this dying vampire, but the one I was looking for.

"Where is he?" I thrust the T-shirt under his nose. "Where is he?"

He laughed, blood burbling out of the neck wound. "You will never find him."

"Tell me and I'll end you quickly."

"Go to hell." It came out more as a gurgle, but I got the message.

With a grin, I thrust the knife home. "You first."

Chapter Thirteen

Fortunately, I wasn't far from the hotel, so I headed back across the park. I flipped my jacket inside out, which looked ridiculous, but covered most of the blood. Unfortunately, I couldn't avoid Francois, the hotel concierge, who apparently worked the front desk practically twenty-four/seven.

"Oh, my, my," he said in his heavy French accent with a gasp, "Mademoiselle Bailey! What has happened to you? You are all-over blood!" He rushed across the lobby of the hotel, exuding distress and flapping his hands wildly. Well, *rushed* might be overstating it. It was more like he minced swiftly. "Are you injured?"

"No, I'm fine, Francois. There was an accident, but—"

A string of French interrupted me, accompanied by more wild hand gestures as he hustled me around the corner and out of sight of other guests. "Mademoiselle Bailey, I am the manager of this hotel! What has happened, it is a travesty! Something must be done! This is no good! I will take care of everything!" Every word was punctuated with exclamation. I swear the man made me exhausted just listening to him.

"I thought you were the concierge."

"Pardon?"

"The concierge."

"Well"—he clapped his hands together and looked grim— "that is true. I was concierge. But I am also night manager!"

"Right. Well, I sort of need to go get cleaned up."

"But of course, of course." He shooed me toward the elevator. "You must clean up right away! If there is anything you need, anything at all, I am here. For you." He clasped his hands together dramatically.

"Thanks. I'll remember that."

Fortunately, the elevator doors slid shut before he could get any more carried away.

As soon as I got into my room, I stripped off my clothes. Most likely ruined, though I hoped the jacket could be saved.

As I turned the shower to scalding and locked the door behind me, it all came crashing down on me: my desperation to find my own killer, my lack of success with Julia's case, and most of all, everything that had happened with Jack. I could no longer hold back my pain over him. Once in the shower, I slid to the floor and let the tears come.

Chapter Fourteen

I didn't sleep the rest of the night. When the sun finally edged its way over the horizon, I threw on some clothes and headed for Hyde Park. I hoped a good, fast walk would burn some of the edge off the anger and hurt I still felt and hopefully allow the hotel maid time to get rid of the evidence of my night with Jack.

Gods, I was such an idiot. I'd let Jack do this to me not once, but twice. I guess this time it really was fool me twice.

I pressed my fist hard against my breastbone, as though the pressure could somehow hold back everything I was feeling. Because under all the anger was pain, burning through my gut like acid. I felt like throwing up. Anger is so much easier to deal with than heartache, but heartache will eat you alive if you let it.

I managed to get a short way into the park before the anger burned out, and I dropped onto a park bench. I swallowed hard, willing myself not to cry. Vampire hunters do not cry. At least not in public. Especially not over a stupid man without the sense the gods gave a chicken.

Hot tears trickled down my cheeks. *Dammit, not again.* I swiped them away, but that didn't stop them from coming. It was a good thing I hadn't bothered with makeup.

I don't know how long I sat there, collar turned against the chill wind, wrapped in my own misery. Kabita found me a little while later. She sat down beside me, stretching her legs out in front of her and crossing her ankles, looking for all the world like she was about to take a morning nap. For a long time, neither of us said anything.

"Jack is an asshole."

That startled a bark of laughter from me. "Preach it." I shifted so I could see her face. "You know what happened?"

"Of course I know. Your room is next to mine. I wouldn't say I heard everything, but I certainly heard enough."

I felt myself blushing.

"I was worried. After last time."

"You were right to be worried."

"Listen, Morgan"—she still didn't touch me, but her presence was like a warm blanket wrapping around my heart, smoothing away the anger and the hurt—"Jack is messed up. You know that, I know that. Apparently, nine hundred years doesn't cure a person of testosterone poisoning."

That made me smile. "Guess not." And Jack had more than most. He'd been a Templar Knight, for crying out loud. Not exactly the sitting-by-the-fire-with-a-good-book type.

"He's scared, you know. He's a warrior, always has been, and the last woman he loved was murdered. He couldn't save her, for all his skills, and now he's got you and he doesn't know how to deal with it."

I thought on that for a moment. It made sense. In fact, it made a lot of sense. But it didn't make me feel any better.

"Yeah, well, life is shit, but wallowing in it doesn't do anyone any good." I stared at the toes of my boots.

"You're right about that. Life is for living, and it's the bad stuff that makes the good stuff so good. We know that, but Jack's forgotten it. Nearly a thousand years of living sort of takes the immediacy out of things. He thinks he's got all the time in the world to deal with this. To deal with you."

I didn't tell her that he might be right. That I might be a sunwalker too. I hadn't even admitted it to myself yet; I wasn't about to admit it to Kabita, no matter that she was my best friend.

"That still doesn't change the fact that he ripped my heart out and stomped on it. Again."

A little girl with sunshine hair tripped by, holding on to her mother with one pudgy hand and a bright-red lollipop with the other. She beamed at me, and I couldn't help but smile back despite the pain in my heart. I wondered if I'd have kids one day.

I indulged myself in a little fantasy, imaging what Jack and my child would have looked like. A little girl, maybe, with sun-streaked hair and ocean-blue eyes. Little nerdy glasses like Inigo...

Inigo? What the heck? I shook my head slightly.

Kabita stood up. "Yeah, and he'll keep doing it if you let him. I don't think he knows if he's coming or going. He wants you, but he can't deal with the guilt, so he'll keep coming back and then freaking out. You've got to be the big brave adult and tell him to step off until he gets his act together."

"I did."

"Then you've got to mean it."

I knew she was right. It was time to stop dancing around with Jack and move on. He would probably never be entirely out of my life, what with all this Atlantean weirdness, but maybe he could be out of my heart. He just wasn't good for me. Like those candies that are lovely and sweet at first and then hit you with a center full of sourness. Still, the thought of him not being mine, not being with me...The pain was almost a physical ache. And hard on that was the bitter taste of loneliness.

I stood up too. "Enough about Jack. I'll get over it, and him. We've got more important things to worry about." Easy to say. Not so easy to do. But damn if I wouldn't try.

Kabita nodded, and we began walking along the wide path. The park was starting to fill up. It was the weekend, after all. A couple of preteens zoomed by on roller skates, followed by an older man on a bike. A young couple pushing a stroller passed us, eyes glued on each other and glazed with love. Part of me wanted to coo, but the other part felt like someone just thrust an ice pick through my heart.

"Anything else new?" Kabita asked.

I was happy to get off the subject of Jack, so I told her about my dream of the dragon. "It was really strange. It felt real, almost more like a memory than a dream, but I haven't been to Hadrian's Wall in years, and I've certainly never met a dragon."

Kabita paused, a funny look on her face.

"Kabita, are you OK?"

She waved me off. "Yes, yes, I'm fine. I was just thinking of something else. Listen, you haven't forgotten our appointment with Ben Landry today, have you?"

I blinked at the sudden change of topic. "No." I totally had. "Of course not. He might know something important. Maybe something about Julia's research."

"Exactly. It's nearly ten. He should be at home now."

I followed her to the taxi stand wondering what was going on in that head of hers. I knew there was more there than met the eye, but as usual with Kabita, she'd tell me when she was good and ready.

∽

Ben Landry lived in a fifth-floor flat in one of the slightly dodgier parts of town. There was no elevator, so we took the stairs. Good thing I stay in shape or I might have died. Well, not literally, of course.

The air inside the stairwell was close and stuffy, reeking of garlic and curry spices and stale urine. There were a few bare bulbs hanging from the ceiling, but they weren't on and I didn't see a switch. Only a tiny grime-covered window on each landing shed a bit of light. It was also a good thing I had excellent night vision, or I could have wound up falling on my ass.

Kabita rapped on Ben's door. We heard shuffling on the other side and then, "Who is it?" His voice was a bit hoarse, like he'd been asleep. Or crying.

"Kabita Jones. Julia's cousin."

I heard a chain rattle, then a slide of the dead bolt and the door swung open. Ben Landry was just as tall and slender as I'd remembered. Up close, I discovered he was better looking than I'd realized. Cute in a kind of geeky way, with really pretty hazel eyes and ridiculously thick black lashes, but his eyes were rimmed in red. Crying, then.

Drinking too, by the smell of him. Though he seemed sober enough.

He smiled at us, and there was sadness behind the smile. "Come in, please." He stepped back so we could enter.

Ben's flat was pretty much what I'd expect of a single guy, but a lot cleaner. Spartan furnishings and zero decoration. Surprisingly, there was no TV. The only things he appeared to have spent money on were a bank of computers along one wall and a really snazzy desk chair.

"Welcome. Can I get you some tea? Coffee?"

We each murmured our thanks and asked for coffee. He waved us to the kitchen table while he tinkered with the kettle.

"Listen, Ben, I'm going to cut to the chase here." Kabita's tone was calm, no-nonsense. "What was your relationship with Julia?"

A spoon clunked against the side of a mug, as though she'd caught him off guard. "I promised her I wouldn't say anything. She didn't want people to know."

"She's dead, Ben." I kept my tone soft and comforting. I guess we were playing good cop, firm cop. "Whatever you tell us can't hurt her anymore."

He closed his eyes, and his shoulders slumped even more. I hadn't known that was possible. With a sigh, he picked up the tray of drinks and brought it to the table. There were only two chairs, so he wheeled over his computer chair and sat.

I held back a smile as he handed me a mug. It had a bright-red background with a white crown and the words *Keep Calm and Carry On*. One of my favorite Briticisms, it never ceases to amuse me.

"Julia and I"—his voice broke a little—"we'd been seeing each other for about six months. We were in love." The last he said a little defensively, as though he thought we wouldn't believe him.

"And?" Kabita prompted.

"She made me promise to keep it a secret." He shrugged and took a sip of his coffee. "I couldn't blame her. With what was going on at MI8, even being friends with me was a bad idea."

I frowned. "What do you mean?"

His jaw clenched. "Ever since I heard about MI8, I've wanted to join. It's all I ever wanted to do, but I knew I'd have to hide my true self if I wanted to work there."

"Why?" I had a feeling I knew.

"I'm a witch."

I watched Kabita's knuckles turn white as she clenched her mug. Her voice was a little hoarse as she asked her next question. "How did you get away with it?"

"I'm essentially latent. I have almost zero power. I can cast a minor finding spell, but that's about it. It was easy enough to bury it, since I rarely use it anyway. The only thing truly witchlike about me is my religion, and they can't ask about that. So I don't tell. I keep it hidden."

"Someone found out?" she prodded.

"They must have. We'd just started seeing each other when Julia found a memo from her uncle ordering MI8's internal investigators to open a case on me. She was afraid that if Mr. Jones discovered we were seeing each other, it would be worse." He stared into his cup, swallowing hard. "She also thought that as long as nobody knew we were together, she'd have a better chance of protecting me."

"Did it work?" she asked.

"It must have. Now she's gone, and I'm on suspension pending investigation."

The irony of an agency devoted to studying and understanding the supernatural refusing to allow admittance to witches did not escape me. There was something hinky about Alister's obsession with witches, especially in light of his own daughter's heritage. As far as I was concerned, being descended from a witch hunter wasn't a good enough reason.

"Do you know what Julia was working on before she died?" I changed the subject. While it sucked what Alister was doing, it wasn't what we were there for.

Ben shook his head. "No idea. She wouldn't talk about it. She'd just write everything in that little notebook of hers. She assured me that, once she had proof, she'd tell me everything, but she didn't want to put me in danger." He heaved a sigh. "As if I wasn't screwed already."

"We found the notebook, but it's in code. Do you know how to read it? This could be really important."

"No idea, I'm afraid. All she said was that it was written in a language older than time, the language of fire." He gave a little laugh. "I have no clue what she was talking about."

I was afraid I did. Kabita and I exchanged looks. There was only one language I knew of that was sometimes referred to as the "language of fire." It was the ancient tongue of the dragons.

Chapter Fifteen

"You know anyone who speaks dragon?" Kabita asked.

We were standing outside Ben Landry's building. I didn't know about Kabita, but I was certainly feeling a little shell-shocked. I gave her a slightly wobbly grin. "Strangely enough, I do know someone."

She grinned back. "Well, then, let's call the lady."

Sandra answered on the third ring. "The Dragon's Den. How may I help you?" her voice rang out cheerily.

"Hey, Sandra. It's Morgan Bailey. I have a small favor."

"Of course, Morgan. How can I help you?"

"I don't suppose you know anyone who can read dragon tongue?"

The pause was what one might refer to as lengthy.

"Sandra?"

"I'm still here."

"Can you help us? It's important."

"Will this help you keep your promise?" Her voice held a slight edge of demand. Not pushy, just reminding me I'd given my word.

"Yes."

"I can't read it," she admitted. "But I might know someone who can help. I'll call you later, all right?"

"OK, thanks. I appreciate this, Sandra."

"I take it she can help?" Kabita started walking toward the tube station, and I followed.

"Yeah, sounds like she knows somebody."

"If she's anything like Cordelia, I have no doubt of it."

We both smirked at each other. Cordelia is a wonderful person, but she knows some really strange people. Then again, so do I.

We split up outside the tube station at Oxford Circus. Kabita wanted to do some shopping, and I'd rather give myself a paper cut and pour lemon juice on it. I hate shopping even at the best of times, and Oxford Street is far from the best, with its crowded sidewalks and hordes of gawking tourists. Sharp elbows are pretty much a requirement.

Instead, I decided to head over to the British Museum. I've always loved it there. My favorite is the Egyptian Room. Unfortunately, unless you hit it either first thing in the morning or last thing at night, it is an absolute nightmare of screaming schoolchildren and photographer wannabes.

Instead, I wormed my way through the crowd around the Rosetta Stone and into the Greek wing. Parts of the Greek exhibition are popular, but the sheer number of artifacts on display means that visitors rarely get much farther than a cursory view of the initial items, leaving many areas tourist-free, quiet, and cool. Especially since it was off-season.

I found one such area and sank down onto the nearest bench. The marble underfoot was slick and cool, the bench perfectly carved to suit my height. A couple of artist types had their camp chairs set up in front of a fresco and were sketching away, but I didn't mind. They were quiet. I stretched out and let my eyes fall on a particularly hideous statue of some Greek deity or other. I looked like I was contemplating the artwork instead of zoning out. Frankly, I needed a break.

My phone vibrated in my front pocket. I pulled it out and hit the call button. "Hello?" I kept my voice low, even though I was in a museum, not a library. No use pissing off the artists. It wasn't like I had a badge I could flash. Kabita has been trying to get Trevor to give us badges, but the Environmental Protection Agency—which is where the Supernatural Regulatory Agency hangs its hat—isn't buying it. We are private citizens, as far as they are concerned.

"Morgan? Why are you whispering?"

Inigo. My palms got a little sweaty, and my heart picked up speed, thumping away in my chest. Why oh why does my libido insist on going into overdrive every time I hear his voice? Especially after what had just happened with Jack.

"I'm in a museum."

"Uh...OK. Should I call back?"

"No, it's fine," I assured him. "What's up?"

"Listen, Kabita told me about your dream."

Shit. What was with people sharing my business all over the place? First Eddie tattling on me to Jack, and now Kabita over-sharing with Inigo. And why would Kabita be sharing my dreams with Inigo, anyway? It wasn't like she ever had before.

"It was just a dream. No biggie." I tilted my head back and stared at the frescoed ceiling. I wondered vaguely who thought up the whole idea of decorating a ceiling. I sort of got it for a bedroom, but otherwise?

"I think maybe it's more than a dream." There was an odd edge to his voice, which made me sit up straighter.

I was quiet for a moment. Sometimes Inigo knows stuff. Stuff he shouldn't in the normal scheme of things. "OK, what do you think it is?"

He sighed, and I could almost see him raking his long artist's fingers through his golden hair.

"I think it's a warning."

"Like a psychic thing?"

"Maybe. Or it might be a subconscious thing. I think maybe your mind is trying to tell you something you already know."

"Like what?" I forgot I was supposed to be keeping it down and raised my voice. The artists turned and glared at me. A museum guard peered around the statue, a frown on his wide face. I mouthed, *Sorry*. The guard shook his head, clearly exasperated. At least he didn't kick me out.

"Like the fact the dragons had nothing to do with Julia's death, but her death had something to do with them..."

Which made sense in a warped and twisted way, because someone sure as hell wanted it to look like dragons were responsible; I just couldn't figure out why. I had a feeling that once we answered the why, we'd figure out the who.

"It also happens," he continued, "that I think what this dragon hunter Sandra told you about has something to do with it. You need to find out more."

"I agree with you. Now I gotta go before they throw me out of here."

"Fine. Morgan?"

"Yeah?"

"Be careful."

I grinned. "Always."

There was laughter in his voice. "Liar."

I smiled as I pressed End and slid the phone back into my pocket. As usual, talking to Inigo had made me feel better. He was like my own personal ray of sunshine.

I glanced up at the ugly statue, my smile turning to a frown. It was time to have a chat with Alister Jones. This time the gloves were coming off.

∽

MI8 headquarters is located in an innocuous-looking building near Hyde Park Corner. In fact, it looks just like the dozens of other Georgian buildings lining both sides of the street. Some are private homes or discreet boutique hotels, while others house the consulates and embassies of smaller nations. I'd been in more than a few of them while on business back in the day.

"You sure you want to do this? I can go in on my own. He can't get mad at you if I'm the one up in his face."

Kabita shook her head. "No. I'm never going to be what Dad wants. It's time I stop pretending otherwise." She squared her shoulders and headed up the wide steps. "And it's time he told the truth."

I certainly agreed with that. I followed her through the front door, noting the discreetly placed security cameras and the neatly disguised fingerprint scanner. It may have looked like any other building, but the place was wrapped up nearly as tight as the crown jewels.

The lobby wasn't much to get excited about. It looked more or less like the entryway in any nice house of the era. The floor was a simple black-and-white check with a small hall table in dark wood topped by a vase of exotic flowers. A carved wood staircase stretched up to the next floor and closed doors bracketed either side of the entrance. I couldn't see any additional cameras, but I'd bet the bank they were there.

We didn't bother trying the doors or attempting to climb the staircase. Instead, we waited quietly, if not calmly.

Five minutes later, the door to the left swung open, and Kabita's eldest brother stepped out. "Hello, girls. Nice to see you again." He gave Kabita a quick hug and me a kiss on the cheek.

"Dex, we're here to see Dad."

"Yeah. Figured. You've got that determined look. Come on up." He led the way up the stairs and down a short hall to what looked like an ordinary door. He fiddled with what I assumed was a light switch but turned out to be a keypad complete with retina scanner. Damn, these people were serious about security.

The rest of the house looked like any classic Georgian home, with beautiful moldings and modest chandeliers, but what lay on the other side of that door was a computer geek's wet dream.

Everything in the room was sleek, slick, and modern. Every desk had a top-of-the-line computer kitted out with every whistle and bell you could imagine. Giant screens lined the walls showing maps and photos and stats. It was like walking into NASA's control center. Insane.

We passed through the open area to another security door, this one without the camouflage. Another scan, another password, and we were following Dex down yet another hall to a plain white door on the end marked *A. Jones*.

Showtime.

Alister was just as suave as ever. He stood to greet us, holding out his hand. I shook it. Kabita didn't say a word. Alister didn't even flinch.

"Ladies, to what do I owe this pleasure?" The way he said it made it clear that this was anything but a pleasure.

I glanced at Kabita. She nodded.

"We're here for the truth," I said.

An eyebrow went up. "The truth? About what, exactly?"

"About dragon hunters, exactly," Kabita snapped. "You told us there weren't any more."

He leaned back in his chair, calmly folding his hands on the wide desk in front of him. "Yes, that is so. There hasn't been a dragon hunter born in generations."

Kabita leaned forward, her face a mask of fury. "You lie."

"Excuse me?"

"You heard me," she hissed. "Why are you lying?"

He leaned forward, his face hard. "I don't care what you think about me, but let me make one thing clear. There are no dragon hunters."

I opened my mouth, but Kabita shook her head. She clearly thought we'd have no luck with Alister. She was probably right.

"No dragon hunters, huh?" I kept my voice light.

"No." The smile he gave me was just this side of smarmy.

"Fine. Tell me this. Why are you persecuting Ben Landry?" I had to admit I felt a bit smug at the startled look on his face. He obviously hadn't expected us to go there.

His jaw went tight. "MI8's investigation of Mr. Landry is none of your concern."

"That's where you're wrong." Kabita's voice was just as hard as her father's. "I'm making it my business. You screwed up my life. I'll be damned if I let you screw up his."

I wanted to give her a standing ovation. Instead, I crossed my arms over my chest and watched. I figured Kabita's accusation wasn't going to go down well with Alister. I was right.

"Get out." His voice was ice.

Kabita placed both palms flat on her father's desk and leaned forward. "Let me make this very clear, *Dad*. I will not stop until I know the truth. And once I know the truth, I will make it my life's goal to ensure everyone else knows it too."

He began shuffling paperwork, completely ignoring the fact that we were both in the room. I placed my hand on her shoulder, urging her away. I could feel her body trembling with rage, and her face was white.

As we left his office, I could feel her fury like a living thing. The darkness in me roared to the surface. It liked the anger, and it wanted out to play. I grabbed at its metaphorical leash, but it was too fast.

Before I could stop it, it started to boil out of me like an inky cloud. It wasn't visible to most, but I could see it spilling out of the center of my chest. Panic shot through me, nearly freezing me to the spot.

I'd never seen the darkness quite like that before, and it terrified me to my core. For a moment, I had no idea what to do, how to handle it.

With a shake of my head, I brought myself back to earth and, within my mind, grabbed the stream of darkness with both hands. It yanked back against me like a wild horse bucking at the reins, refusing to be broken. I yanked again, to no avail. Sweat beaded my forehead, and fear turned to acid in my veins.

This was it. I was finally going to lose control.

Suddenly, it retracted inside me, all on its own. I had no idea why it had decided to cooperate, and its compliance scared me almost more than its resistance. I clearly wasn't the one in control here.

My palms burned. I rubbed them up and down my pant legs, and my hands shook ever so slightly. Kabita needed to calm down, and calm down now, before her freak-out caused my wonderful newfound abilities to really act up. If it decided to take over, there was clearly nothing I could do to stop it.

Fortunately, I didn't have to worry about it. Dex met us in the hallway, distracting Kabita. "Follow me."

He led us back through the noisy room with the computers, out through the security door, and into the hall. Before we got to the stairs, he opened a door on the right that led into the world's smallest office. I actually had to stand in the doorway, since there wasn't enough room for the three of us.

This room was nothing like the sleek offices behind the security door, all shining and slick. A metal desk that had seen far better days was crammed up against one wall and occupied by a computer that looked older than I did. The rest of the space, what there was of it, was overrun by two enormous filing cabinets. Stacks of books and files were everywhere.

Dex opened the bottom drawer of his desk, pulled out a bottle of whiskey, and splashed two fingers into the bottom of a coffee mug. Silently, he handed it to Kabita. She swallowed it in one gulp. My throat burned in sympathy.

"I take it things didn't go well with Dad."

"You take that right." It was practically a snarl.

I leaned against the wall while Kabita attempted to pace the room. I wished her luck. She had all of about two steps to go in any direction.

Dex sighed and ran his fingers through thick black hair. "Listen, K, I don't know how much I can help, but I'll do what I can. We all will. Adam and Adler are itching to help. What do you want us to do?"

Kabita looked a little surprised at Dex's offer. Then she smiled. Obviously, she hadn't realized just how much her brothers had her back.

I wondered what it would be like to have brothers to protect and look after me. Would my life have been different if I'd had siblings? It was hard to imagine having that kind of relationship with anyone. Though a tiny piece of me wished I did.

No use crying over what couldn't be, right?

"What about the archives?" I piped up.

"Good idea," Kabita said. "Julia was supposedly going through the archives, looking at old files before she died. Can you get us in, Dex?"

He rolled his eyes. "You don't ask much, do you? I can get you in, but it won't be easy."

Kabita was quiet for a moment. "Listen, Dex, you don't have to do this. I know Dad's lifelong obsession with destroying the supernatural has gone into overdrive. If he catches you, you're in deep shit."

"You worry about yourself, K. I'll be fine. I'm going to attempt damage control, but right now, Dad's got the power of MI8 behind him. There's only so much I can do. I'll do what I can, though. You're my sister." The finality in his voice told me *end of story*.

Dex would help as much as he could, no matter what problems it might cause him.

I watched a little enviously as Dex and Kabita hugged and did the cheek kissy thing. Then she and I slipped out of MI8 and down the street. I didn't relax until we were out of sight of the building, and even then, I felt itchy all over. Like I was being watched.

I glanced at the nearest CCTV camera. They are all over the city. It makes London safer, but it also means that doing my job is a heck of a lot harder. Fortunately, I know where the blind spots are.

"Do you think he's watching us?" I asked Kabita.

She didn't pretend not to know who I was talking about. "What do you think?"

"Then how on earth are we going to get into that building without your father catching us?" *And locking us up for good, no doubt.*

The smile she gave me was just a little creepy. "Trust me, he'll never know we were there."

Looked like Kabita had decided to play dirty.

Chapter Sixteen

The phone call came shortly after midnight. We were waiting in a green space across the street from MI8.

"Yeah. Uh-huh. Got it." Kabita switched off her phone. "That was Dex. Adam and Adler have the keycard ready. After that, we're going to have to bullshit our way."

I glanced up at the Georgian building. It was mostly empty now, and there were only a couple of windows still lit. "Looks like your dad's still in there."

She frowned. "Yeah. Probably best we avoid him."

You think? I gave her an eye roll and tugged my cap lower over my eyes.

Dex had stopped by the hotel earlier and dropped off a couple of outfits and a plastic key card. It wasn't an official MI8 key card, since those were all accounted for, but Adam and Adler had hacked the system so it would work just for tonight.

We strolled across the street. To any watching eyes, we looked like a couple of maintenance types taking a leisurely evening stroll. The baggy coveralls and ball caps turned us into unisex nonentities.

Nobody looked twice at the cleaners.

I dug the card Dex had given us out of my pocket and swiped it across the sensor. Nothing.

I glanced at Kabita. She shrugged.

I blew out a breath. If this didn't work, we were back to square one. I swiped the card again.

This time a green light appeared over the fingerprint scanner. I flipped up the cover on the scanner, and Kabita pressed her thumb against the panel. There was a small clunking sound as the door lock released. Adam and Adler had come through. They'd swapped Kabita's prints in MI8's records for the real cleaner's, and they'd erase them later, leaving no trace we'd ever been there.

We pushed our way into the lobby. Straight ahead were the stairs leading up to the floors above. On either side of the lobby were single doors leading, I assumed, to hallways with more rooms.

I couldn't see any security, but I knew they were watching. Sure enough, before we could take another step, a security guard came hurrying down the stairs in front of us.

"Evening, ladies. New, aren't you?" The security guard looked like he should be in the WWE. Thick muscles strained at his polyester uniform, and he walked with that strut men have when they know they could beat the ever-loving crap out of just about anyone they come across.

If I opened my mouth, we were goners. There were plenty of Americans in London, but the coincidence would be a little too much if Alister caught wind of it. Fortunately, Kabita spoke up.

"Hello, yes, we are very, very new."

It was all I could do not to wet myself laughing. She'd put on the heaviest Indian accent I'd ever heard. The guard didn't even bat an eyelash.

"Your friend doesn't talk much."

"Oh, she is not speaking English. I try to teach her, but it is taking time, you know?" She bobbed her head from side to side. Damn, she was good.

"Really. Damn foreigners. Ought to learn English if they want to live here." He glared at me.

I pretended to look intimidated. In actuality, I was furious. I'd have liked nothing more than to punch the bigot right in his smug face.

Kabita edged us across the lobby, keeping up the cheerful immigrant act. "You are right, sir. Of course! That is why I teach her."

We strode toward the door on the right, and I waved my card over the next sensor. Moving like you have every right to be there is the key to not getting caught breaking and entering. But if the door didn't open, we were going to have problems, especially with the big-ass security guard breathing down our necks.

This time the door popped open without hesitation. The hall on the other side of the door was short and carpeted in an ugly gray.

"Last door on the left," Kabita said under her breath, as the door shut on the hovering security guard.

I gave a slight nod, and we proceeded down the hall. The last door on the left was unlocked and proved to be nothing more exciting than your average, ordinary maintenance closet stacked to the ceiling with rolls of toilet paper and bottles of cleaning products.

The room was too small for both of us to enter at one time, so Kabita wheeled the cleaning cart into the hallway, and we both started loading it up. We used our trips into the closet to hide our conversation as much as possible.

"Dex said the door to the archives is at the other end of the building, basement level. There aren't any gaps in security there, so we're going to have to figure something out."

"OK," I whispered back. "I have an idea. I'll see if it will work when we get there."

"Fine. But it will look suspicious if we go straight to that part of the building."

"So, we start at this end. There are only a couple of rooms."

She nodded, so I slowly wheeled the cart to the first door. I angled my body slightly so anyone watching us on CCTV couldn't see the card as I swiped it. I shouldn't have worried. The door opened immediately. Obviously, the twins had gotten the hang of things.

We made quick work of the two rooms. The cleaning company was probably going to get complaints, which would no doubt confuse them, since their services for the evening had been canceled by Kabita, posing as the administration manager. We moved out into the lobby.

The security guard had disappeared back upstairs, so Kabita hurried us up to the door on the left-hand side of the lobby. The door popped open, and we slid through.

We both sucked in a deep breath, but we weren't out of the woods yet. I pushed the cart to the end of the hall while Kabita kept up her ridiculous impression routine, talking loud and fast and making wild hand gestures, just in case someone was watching.

The door to the basement where the archives were kept was dead ahead, in clear view of the CCTV camera. Fortunately, there was a door perpendicular to it, which led into the women's bathroom.

I angled the cart in front of the women's room so that it blocked the view of anyone coming or going from the bathroom—if, that is, the person were crawling. Which was exactly what I planned to do.

Kabita propped open the bathroom door as I grabbed an armload of toilet paper rolls. Inside the bathroom, I dropped the rolls and handed her the key card.

"OK," I said, "here's my plan. You walk out there and stand at the cart. Rustle around like you can't find something, and make sure the cart is angled to block the view of the archive door as much as possible. Use the feather duster to clean the camera pointing at the door so I can crawl to the archive door and slip inside. Then you can clean the bathroom while I see what I can find in the archives. Security will think I'm still in the bathroom with you."

"OK, fine. How about I give you fifteen minutes; then I'll do it again so you can crawl out."

Fifteen minutes wasn't a lot of time, but there wasn't much we could do about it. Muscle Head knew where we were, and even though I was sure he'd bought our story, we didn't want to rouse his suspicions. Any more than fifteen minutes and he'd be down wanting to know what we were up to.

Our plan went off flawlessly, and five minutes later, I was standing at the top of the stairs leading to the basement level that housed the archives. I started down into the belly of the whale, so to speak.

Honestly, I had no idea where to begin. The archives were a mess. Sure, there were plenty of shelves with neatly labeled boxes, but the labels made no sense to me. They'd used something that looked a bit like the Dewey decimal system, and without the key, I had no idea how to decipher it. On top of that, there were additional unlabeled boxes stacked haphazardly around the room and topped with stacks of files and papers. There was a single long table obviously meant for sorting through the archive boxes, but it too was covered with dusty files.

"Crap." *Where to start?* I only had fifteen minutes to figure out what Julia had been researching down there.

My mind cranked over, running through the possibilities. Julia had been a smart woman. She wouldn't have just left her research for anyone to find. Not that anyone would be able to find anything around here.

I headed to the back of the large room, darting quickly through the shelves and around more piles of boxes. There were a couple of desks shoved up against the far wall and piled just as high with paperwork as the front table had been. Seemed like the perfect place to hide an ongoing investigation.

I flipped through the first stack of files and loose papers. Nothing struck a chord. It was all field status reports and notes on decades-old cases. I went through two more stacks before realizing it was going to take forever at this rate. So I started pulling things randomly from the stacks. File after file, I found nothing but ancient history and equally ancient dust. And then I hit pay dirt.

I pulled a file from the middle of a stack on the desk and flipped it open. *Bingo.* Inside the file was a hot-pink sticky note with some writing on it. I recognized Julia's handwriting from her journal. This was definitely what I'd been looking for.

A quick scan through the rest of the pile yielded no results, so I unzipped my coverall and stuffed the file down into the top of my jeans. The coverall was loose, but not loose enough to stand up to close examination.

I checked my watch. Nearly out of time. I scurried back up the steps and waited until my watch hit the right time. I pushed open the door just as Kabita started up her dusting routine. I crawled back to the bathroom, and she joined me moments later.

"Did you find anything?"

"Yeah." I unzipped my coverall enough so she could see the file.

"What's in the file?"

"Didn't have time to look. What next?"

"We need to get out of here without tipping off the asshat."

I snorted with laughter at that. "Any ideas?"

She gave me an evil grin. I had a feeling I wasn't going to like this.

"Where are you two going? You haven't finished yet." Muscle Head stormed down the stairs, buttons ready to pop, suspicion written all over his face.

"It is my friend Ingrid. She is ill."

Ingrid? Seriously?

I sagged a little more against Kabita. She grunted under my weight and gave me a look that told me I was going to pay for it later.

The guard took a step back. "What's she got?"

"I am not knowing. One minute she is fine. The next…" She made a sound like somebody throwing up.

Muscle Head frowned. "You have to be joking."

"Oh, no, I am not joking, sir. I need to be getting her home. Here." She thrust me at the guard, and I sagged tragically in his arms.

"I am being right back, sir. Need to be putting this away." She waved at the cleaning cart before disappearing through the door.

The guard must have gotten a whiff of me. "Jesus, you stink." He made a face and shoved me down onto the first step. "You'd better not be contagious."

I made a gagging sound like I was about to throw up. Muscle Head jumped back about a foot, swearing up a storm. It was all I could do not to burst out laughing.

The thing about making a lie convincing is to cover all your bases. Most people are good at thinking about sound and sight, but they forget smell. Nothing will get a guy like Muscle Head to back off like the smell of puke.

I am not an advocate for self-induced vomiting. It's a waste of perfectly good food. But as a disguise, it totally works.

Kabita came bustling back through the door, heaved me off my feet (I made a few dry heaving sounds, just for effect), and got me out the front door of MI8, pronto. "Not to worry, sir," she shouted at Muscle Head, "we be sending someone to finish cleaning. Not to worry."

And we disappeared into the night with Muscle Head staring after us, looking slightly green around the gills.

თ

The first thing I did when we got back to the hotel was brush my teeth. The second thing I did was gargle with mouthwash. Twice. The third thing I did was ask Kabita about the file. She'd hidden it in her own coverall so Muscle Head wouldn't feel it when she threw me at him.

She flipped through the pages as I collapsed on the bed. "Looks like we've got the information we were looking for. These are the birth records of a dragon hunter."

"You can know someone is a hunter from birth?" That was something I hadn't known.

"Not exactly. You can track family lines to find possible hunters, but the abilities don't usually manifest until close to puberty. He must have been tracking her mother when she gave birth."

"Let me see that."

She handed me the file.

"So, Sandra was right. There is a dragon hunter on the loose, and MI8 is covering it up." And apparently Julia had found out about it.

"I don't think MI8 are the ones covering it up. I think it's my father behind the cover-up. It's his style."

"But why?" There was so much crazy going on the possibilities were endless.

"No idea. What do the files say, exactly?"

I leaned back against the pillows as I scanned the documents. "This one is a birth certificate. It looks like a girl was born on the first of June twenty-three years ago right here in London. She was given the name Dara Boyd. No father's name, and the mother's name is redacted."

"Excuse me? Redacted?"

"Yep. As is pretty much everything else. I seriously doubt Boyd is her real name."

She thought for a moment. "I doubt she uses Dara anymore. She most likely has an entirely new identity. What else?"

"It looks like MI8 kept pretty close tabs on her. There are school records, names and addresses of foster families, even medical and dental records." I took out my cell phone and started snapping photos of the documents for future reference. "There are notes on her friends. She didn't have many. No boyfriends. One girlfriend." I squinted at the pink sticky note next to the woman's name. "An address. I'd bet anything it was the girlfriend's."

"Maybe she knows something," Kabita suggested.

I shrugged. "Maybe, though, from what we know of hunters, Dara may not have been aware of her nature. At least until she was older. Even then, I doubt she knew exactly what she was."

"Unless someone told her."

There was that. I flipped to the last page of the file. "Huh. The records end shortly after her eighteenth birthday."

"They stopped tracking her?"

"No." I shook my head. "It looks like they lost her. She disappeared off the grid."

"Impossible." She snagged the file out of my hands, sinking down onto the desk chair to peruse it. She bit her lower lip as she read. "She had help."

"How do you know? Maybe she just moved or something."

"No. MI8 knew what she was, and they were keeping very close tabs on her. It wasn't just a matter of surveillance. They had her tagged."

"What? Like on those wildlife shows where they stick a GPS in the ear of a rabbit or something?"

She grimaced. "Pretty much. Any suspected hunter born on British soil is tracked that way from birth through an implant. Those who show promise as hunters are recruited. Those who don't are still kept under surveillance—permanently."

"Geez. Glad I wasn't born here." I touched my ear. "Uh, they didn't put a chip in me when I was in the hospital, did they?"

She gave me an eye roll. "Don't be ridiculous." She went back to reading the file.

"I'm serious, Kabita. Did they chip me?"

She was quiet a moment. "My father wanted to, but you're American, and Americans don't chip their hunters."

"Like that would stop Alister."

She snorted. "It didn't. Aunt Angeline did."

Ah. The aunt who'd saved me from MI8's tender mercies. "Thank the gods for Aunt Angeline."

She grinned at that before returning to the file. "They'd have never just let Dara Boyd go. Not unless…" She flipped through the file, a frown forming. "It looks like the computer system the chips upload to was shut down for routine maintenance, only the backup system didn't kick in. By the time it came back online, she was gone. I'd bet anything somebody helped her. Too much of a coincidence."

"MI8 didn't try to find her?"

Her face was grim. "No, they didn't. At least not for very long. Look." She handed the file back, open to a yellow duplicate page.

It was a simple document ordering that the search for Dara Boyd be terminated. It was signed by one Alister Jones.

"Damn."

Breakfast the next morning was a tense one—each of us lost in our own thoughts and each of us still pissed off about Alister. I was pretty grateful he wasn't my father right about then. Honestly, the more I learned about him, the less I liked him.

What I really wanted to know was exactly what game he was playing at and why. Between his crazy witch-hunting obsession and his lying about there being a dragon hunter on the loose, there was definitely something up.

After breakfast, we both needed to burn off some energy, so we took a walk through the streets of Mayfair. The pretty brick buildings with their arched and curlicue facades turn that part of London from an ordinary city into something out of a fairy tale. Or maybe *Mary Poppins*.

The American embassy was mere blocks away, but we didn't go there. Instead, we wound up in the little park just in front of it. Grosvenor Square is a miniplayground for the office drones in the area to picnic and catch some rays—or z's, for that matter—during lunch. But at this time of day, it was nearly empty.

"He'll never tell the truth, you know." It was the first Kabita had spoken since we left the hotel, the first time we'd discussed what we'd found in the files since the previous night.

"Nope," I agreed. "We can hound him from here to eternity, and he won't tell us anything. We're going to have to figure this out on our own."

"And then what?" Her voice was unusually dull.

"Then we do what we have to."

She nodded. "OK."

What else was there to say, really?

"Next step?"

She shook her head as though to clear it. "We need to track this girl. Find out where she is, what she's calling herself, get a description. I think I should have a chat with her girlfriend. What was her name?"

I pulled up the memory of the hot-pink sticky note. "Simone Williams. According to Julia's notes, she was the last person to see Dara before her disappearance. Her last-known address is in Willesden Junction, but she could be anywhere by now."

"I'll get Adam to track her down. I'm going to have a little chat with Simone. She might know something, have seen something. Even if she didn't, she should be able to give me the names of some of the other people in Dara's life."

"Great, while you do that—" I was cut off by the ringtone on my mobile. It was Sandra.

"Morgan, can you come to my shop this afternoon?"

"Sure," I said. "What's up?"

"I've found someone who might be able to translate the diary."

Chapter Seventeen

This time, on my way through Soho, there wasn't a sidhe in sight, which was something of a relief. Thank the gods for small favors. My life was complicated enough without the sidhe.

Sandra's shop was shut, the closed sign dangling in the window. I rapped once and the door swung open. Sandra waved me in, her eyes darting up and down the street as though she were afraid someone was spying on us. I couldn't imagine what she had to be nervous about. Unless her translator was some kind of criminal or something.

"Thank you for coming so quickly, Morgan. It's not good for…my guest to be out among people for very long."

Oh, boy. "Of course. Thanks for helping me. I really appreciate it."

She gave me a look that reminded me there was backbone underneath the sometimes loony exterior. "I'm not doing it for you. I'm doing it for my friends."

What could I say? I nodded and followed her into the back room.

I didn't know what I was expecting. Maybe a cerebral professor type complete with tweed jacket and smoking pipe. The man lounging in Sandra's desk chair was pretty much the exact opposite.

He was big. Really big, with broad shoulders straining at a battered black leather biker jacket. What looked like size sixteen combat boots were propped up on her desk, and the man's massive arms were crossed over his chest. He made Muscle Head, the security guard, look undernourished.

He was handsome; I'd give him that. His cheekbones would make a romance cover model weep with envy.

Sandra started to introduce us, but the man interrupted her. "So, you're the hunter." Sapphire-blue eyes ringed with ink-black lashes the same color as his shoulder-length hair swept over me and dismissed me all in one go.

Oh, no, he didn't. Nobody dismisses Morgan Bailey like some kind of bug. Especially since I had a sneaking suspicion I knew what he was. That voice had invaded my dreams. I'd had no idea until that moment that dragons could take human form, and I wasn't sure I liked the idea.

"So, you're the one who can translate dragon tongue." I sniffed the air. "Barbecue any sheep lately?"

He was out of the chair with a snarl before I could blink. I probably should have backed down, but there isn't anything that irritates me more than a man who treats a woman as inferior. Even if he could, quite literally, eat her in one gulp.

Then his eyes shifted, turned silvery gold, pupils elongating. I realized that it wasn't a gender bias. It was one species treating another as inferior. Much like a human might view a dog. I swallowed hard, but stood my ground.

"Drago, please." Sandra laid a calming hand on his arm. He didn't budge. Not just any dragon, then, but a dragon king. I'd done my reading.

"Drago is your title." I made it a comment, not a question. Meanwhile, I held his eyes with mine. They were familiar, those eyes. Not his specifically, but something about them. My mind tried to catch the thought, but it slid away.

"Yes." His voice was deep and grumbly.

"Do you often play with the dreams of humans?"

Just a hint of a smile played around his mouth. I noted his lips were full and sensual. In human form, he was definitely sexy, but he honestly did nothing for me. It wasn't because he was a dragon, either. I could see the sexy, but I wasn't into it.

"Sometimes I find it is the best way to communicate. Little humans are prone to fits of hysteria when faced with such as I." His voice rose and fell in the odd cadence I remembered from the dream. His speech patterns felt more formal, which I supposed made sense, seeing how English wasn't his first language.

"Well, next time, could you knock first?"

His smile grew wider, and he inclined his head, his pupils slipping back into their human shape. Sandra breathed a sigh of relief. If I were honest, so did I.

"You have something that needs translating?"

"Yeah." I sat down on the folding chair Sandra had pulled out of gods knew where. I slid the diary out of my pocket and laid it on the desk. "This diary was written by a woman called Julia Reynolds."

He nodded and propped a pair of reading glasses on his nose.

I gave him a look. "Seriously? You wear glasses?"

He smirked at me. "We all have our weaknesses, little human. Best not to forget it."

"I never do, believe me."

He flipped through the pages of the diary. "This woman, Julia—she was human?"

"Yes, she worked for MI8."

"Ah, that explains it."

"Explains what?"

"See here." He leaned forward, his finger pointed at a symbol in the diary. His scent caught me by surprise. He smelled like a s'more. I love s'mores.

Thinking of s'mores reminded me of Inigo. Thinking of Inigo got me more than a little hot under the collar. But more than that, it made me feel...happy. Warm. Safe. I cleared my throat and squirmed a little in my chair. "Yeah. What about it?"

"It's very old. We don't use it anymore except, perhaps, in very formal situations." He frowned, flipping through the pages. "This isn't in dragon tongue."

I gave him a doubtful look. "Come on. Those are dragon symbols. Even I know that."

"Yes," he admitted. "They are symbols of the dragon tongue, but this diary is written in English. The dragon symbols are simply a code of sorts."

"You mean she substituted dragon tongue symbols for English words?"

"More like she used the symbols to represent similar English sounds. Many of the symbols are very old and have fallen out of use in the centuries of our exile beyond the wall. My guess would be Julia Reynolds had access to some type of dictionary of symbols, most likely stored at MI8. She used it as you might use hieroglyphs or Morse code, to protect her findings."

He leaned back again. Gods he smelled good. And he was making me hungry. I had the sudden desire to visit Paul's Patisserie for something ridiculously gooey and chocolaty.

"So, can you translate it or not?"

He peered at me over his glasses. "Oh, I can translate it. It may not be exactly as written, but close enough."

"Fine. Can you tell me what Julia was working on before she was murdered?"

"Of course," he said with a shrug. "That is easy. She was trying to find the dragons."

I swear, my mouth dropped open like an idiot.

"Tea, anyone?" Sandra popped her head into the room.

We both nodded. She smiled and popped back to wherever she'd been. I could hear the clinking of china and the slosh of water as she busied herself in what was obviously a kitchen area.

"Does it say why?" I couldn't imagine why Julia had cared about finding dragons. After all, nobody believed they were real anymore, and those who did thought they were all dead.

"It appears she accidentally discovered the truth about our race. When she brought the facts to the attention of her superiors, she was shut down, ordered to keep silent." His finger traced the pages. "Instead, she kept investigating quietly. She came to believe that someone within the organization was using MI8 to further his or her own ends."

"What does that have to do with your people?"

"It is not clear. However, she also determined that the dragon hunters were not extinct, but that there was at least one in existence." He shook his head, strands of inky silken hair sliding over his shoulders. "I do not see how this is possible. Even worse, instead of being trained as a hunter, this one had been spirited away to live in the United States."

Sandra bustled out with a tea tray piled with the requisite tea things and a load of tea biscuits. Drago smiled when he saw the cookies and helped himself to a large handful. I have a weakness for the biscuits myself, so I couldn't blame him. They are just so moreish. There is no way you could eat just one.

"The US?" I picked up the conversation. "You're kidding. Talk about a small world. But why was that a bad thing? And why don't you think it's possible?"

He stared at me for several moments, as though trying to determine whether I was worthy of knowledge. I tried to look studious or innocent or something. I was not sure it worked.

"You've no doubt been told that the dragon hunter ability is genetic and that it appeared out of nowhere."

I nodded. That was exactly what I'd been told. What Alister Jones himself had told me.

"It isn't genetic. It can't be passed from one generation to the next. Each dragon hunter must be created."

I stared at him for a moment. "Excuse me? Created by whom?"

"Centuries ago, the first rogue dragon began slaughtering humans by the hundreds. Horrified, the clans hunted him down and tried to restrain him, but they could not, and so thousands of humans died."

I frowned. "So far, it sounds exactly like the story I was told. Why didn't they kill the rogue?"

"They tried. Unfortunately, he escaped, and this time he hid far too well."

"I still don't understand who created the dragon hunters."

He held up a hand. "Patience."

"Sorry. Go on. Please." My voice was just a little tart.

He smiled a little at that. "The only result of such carnage would, of course, have been war. And war meant the death of millions, possibly even the extinction of either your race or mine. Faced with such a horror, the Drago, my grandfather, created a new creature—dragon hunter."

The dragons had created dragon hunters? My mind stuttered to a halt over that one. "How is that even possible?"

He gave me a look. "There are some secrets I am not prepared to share."

"Fair enough, but why would a dragon hunter succeed where a dragon could not?" It just made no sense to me that a little tiny human could do what an entire clan of dragons couldn't.

"Because dragon hunters don't just hunt and kill rogues; they are also capable of controlling them—with their minds."

Holy shit.

Drago continued. "From time to time, other dragons went rogue, and the dragon hunters were called out. Unfortunately, the dragon hunters did not stop at killing rogue dragons. Their insatiable lust for death drove them to kill even the innocent, and so the human-dragon conflict began, after all. When faced with annihilation, there was only one thing left to do. We built the wall and then withdrew behind it."

He watched me closely. Did he expect me to go ballistic or something? I was just too confused by the whole thing.

"The dragons built the wall? Not Hadrian?"

"Oh, please"—he waved his hand—"as though the Roman Empire ever told the truth about anything. Talk about the world's biggest propaganda machine."

If what he was telling me were true, then nothing in the history books was right. Well, the history books that included dragons—or Romans, for that matter.

"But there were humans behind the wall."

He nodded. "Of course. But these had not been involved in the conflict, and they had no interest in our affairs. They were happy enough to leave us alone if we returned the favor. The Scottish are very pragmatic, after all.

"When the dragon hunters finished killing rogues and started killing the other dragons, my grandfather stopped making dragon hunters. They eventually died out."

"And that's why there haven't been any dragon hunters over the last few centuries," I concluded.

"Correct. This dragon hunter you speak of wasn't made by me. I don't know who and I don't know how they discovered the secret. It is possible she had an ancestor who was a dragon hunter. But someone else made her."

I had a bad feeling I knew who'd been playing God. And he just happened to be my best friend's father. "Shit."

"Exactly."

I sighed and slumped in my chair and took a bite of tea biscuit. The sweet vanilla filled my mouth. "Why on earth would anyone let a dragon hunter run loose like that?"

He gave me a pointed look. "Must I spell it out for you?"

"No. No, not really." There was only one reason to let a dragon hunter loose—to hunt dragons. "What about Julia's murder? You really think someone was trying to stir things up by framing the dragons? Start another war?" A war that would most likely end in the complete annihilation of the dragon race. Not to mention that some pretty bad shit would happen to my own human race.

He laid the diary on the table and leaned back in his chair. Those sapphire eyes of his caught mine, asking, demanding. "That would be my guess. What I want to know, Morgan Bailey, is how you are going to play this."

"Like I always play it," I told him, "on the side of truth."

"No matter the cost? No matter who gets in your way?"

I stood up and snagged the diary off the desk. "The way I look at it, Drago, is that anybody who pulls this kind of bullshit deserves whatever they get." I wasn't about to mention my suspicions just yet. I didn't know Drago, but if it had been me, I'd be out for blood. "We're talking attempted genocide. Not to mention the murder of an innocent woman. That is so not OK." Understatement of the year, but there you go.

A slow smile spread across his too-handsome face. "That's what I like to hear. Perhaps we can work with you, after all." He stood and held out his hand.

As I took it, he pulled me in close, his sweet chocolate-and-marshmallow scent wafting over me, swamping my senses. Heat ripped through my body, and it was just this side of painful. I so wasn't comfortable with the proximity, but he was too strong for me.

His lips brushed against my ear, sending shivers down my spine. And they weren't happy shivers. "Remember, Hunter, the fire is a gift. Do not refuse it lest it eat you."

His voice was rough coals, and his hand wrapped around mine wasn't warm; it was hot, sending flames shooting up my arm and into my body. But I wasn't turned on. There wasn't much in this world I was afraid of anymore, but the man-dragon in front of me wasn't exactly your ordinary monster. I was scared.

Me. The vampire hunter. Scared.

I jerked my hand back and swallowed hard. With a nod, I turned and strode quickly from the shop. I refused to let fear, or the dragon king, get the better of me.

Behind me, Drago laughed.

Darkness had fallen by the time I left the Dragon's Den. The streetlamps cast their mellow orange glow over the cobbled streets of Soho as a drunk couple staggered past me, arms wrapped around each other. I wrinkled my nose. I could smell the reek of alcohol on them.

Laughing, one of the men slammed the other up against a shop wall. I braced myself for action before realizing it wasn't aggression—at least not in a bad way, if the kissing was anything to go by.

I tucked my hands into my jacket pockets and tried not to stare too much as I passed them. An unexpected ping of jealousy hit me out of nowhere. Why couldn't my love life be that simple? A little too much wine and some hot groping on a street corner sounded pretty good to me.

I'd just turned the corner when that tingle gripped the back of my skull, stopping me in my tracks. Vampire. It was downwind, so I couldn't catch a physical scent, and its metaphysical one was murky. Probably thanks to the bombardment of my other senses. Soho isn't exactly a calm place. I knelt down as though to tie my shoelace and carefully slid my blade from its ankle sheath.

"So, little Hunter, we meet again, at last."

He stood a few feet away, wrapped in shadow. I couldn't see his features, but now I could smell him with that odd sense I had—and I'd never forget that voice. It was the voice of the monster who'd murdered me. "You've led me on a merry chase these last few days, Bob."

"Bob?" he sounded amused.

I shrugged. "Sounds good to me."

Fangs flashed in the dim light and a chuckle followed. "You Americans are such an odd bunch. I suppose it comes from living in the wilderness of the colonies all these years."

Was he serious? "You didn't answer my question."

"You didn't ask a question."

"Why have you been following me?"

He sighed. "You are amazingly thick for a hunter. Very disappointing. Especially considering I'm essentially your sire."

"Excuse me?"

This time his smile chilled me to the bones. He took one step closer. "I made you. Without me, you would be languishing in the ordinary. I made you extraordinary."

He was actually trying to take the credit for my becoming a hunter. As if that made his killing me OK. "If you're waiting for me to thank you, you're going to be waiting one hell of a long time."

He shrugged as if to say he had plenty of time. He wouldn't, if I could help it. I adjusted my grip on the knife handle. "Answer me."

A sly smile spread across his face. "I was paid to lead you around London. Distract you. Just for a few days, you understand."

"You ran me all around London for *money*?"

He examined his nails before buffing them on the lapel of his snazzy wool coat. "Living takes money, you know. And I've lived a very long time."

"Well, then let me fix that for you."

I wanted my revenge. I wanted it so bad it was almost an obsession. And that made me hesitate.

Apparently, the darkness had no such qualms. It came in a rush, ramming through me like an ocean wave. The edges of my vision bled black. It shrieked with glee, and it wasn't just the darkness shrieking; it was me.

"Holy goddess," Bob whispered, "what are you?"

"The goddess can't help you now, Bob. No one can." The voice that came out of my mouth was mine and yet not mine. It held the weight of a thousand tombs.

It was as though the darkness had taken over my very being. There was nothing left of me. I was the darkness. And I was glorious.

With sheer force of will, I managed to push the darkness aside just enough so I felt myself again. I no longer felt the overwhelming joy of darkness, which was both a relief and a loss. Now, instead of the darkness completely controlling me, it was like we were side by side within my own body. Yet I knew without a shadow of a doubt the darkness could take over at any moment.

The thought was terrifying, but I pushed it aside. At that moment, I craved revenge more than anything else.

Apparently, Bob decided he wasn't going to sit there and wait to get turned into dog meat. He ran at me. The darkness laughed, and I was across the street and on him faster than a heartbeat.

Bob grabbed a handful of my jacket and used my momentum to swing me around and into the wall. I landed so hard it rattled my teeth. I'd no doubt have some lovely bruises.

He went for my throat, fangs flashing in the dim light, but I brought up one arm and, with strength born of darkness, broke his hold. With my other hand, I got a good grip on his throat. He snarled and I snarled back, lifting the knife and driving it into his stomach and giving the blade a vicious twist.

With a snarl, Bob picked me up and threw me. I flew a good twenty feet before crashing down on the pavement. Something snapped and pain flooded my body, but the darkness growled and shoved it back. I felt nothing but the bliss of darkness, and that frightened me to my very core.

Yet beyond the fear was the knowledge that I needed it. I was injured and tiring, and without it, I would never win. Still, giving in entirely wasn't an option, despite the fact that part of me wanted that more than anything.

The other part of me, the sane part of me, was smart enough to know that was a really bad idea.

The darkness wasn't all power; it was cunning too. I lay, waiting, catching my breath until Bob was within arm's reach. Then I reached out and grabbed his ankle, flipping him into the air and onto his back. He landed with enough force that, if vampires breathed, it would have knocked the wind out of him.

In a flash, I was on top of him, straddling his chest, knife at his throat. The darkness longed to rip his heart out of his chest, and I struggled to hold it back. I needed answers. "Who paid you, Bob?" I could barely hiss out the words past the darkness that was growing stronger and stronger inside me. It wanted to rend and kill, to bathe itself in the vampire's blood. "Who wants me dead?" Because that's what it was. A hit. Whoever hired Bob had to have known that he would try to finish what he'd started.

What they didn't know was that I was no longer easy to kill.

"If I tell you, will you let me go?"

I hesitated for a moment. There was no way I could promise that, but I needed the information. Before I could say a word, the darkness smiled with my mouth. "Of course, Bob."

"Swear it."

"We swear it. On everything we hold dear. If you tell us who hired you, we will let you go." My voice had a weird double echo— part me and part the darkness. Deep inside, I felt a thrill of terror.

"Fine. It was a woman called Jade. A hunter, but not like you."

"Very good, Bob," the darkness said with my mouth, my voice. It was as though I were watching from the corner as the darkness completely engulfed my body. "Thank you for telling us." The blade bit into his neck, spilling a thin trickle of blood.

Fear flashed across a face that might have once been handsome. "You promised."

"Of course we did, Bob. And we keep our promises. We will let you go back to the dust which made you," the darkness hissed.

"No! Please!"

"Sorry, Bob." Without warning, the darkness was gone and in its place was fire. Fire so hot it burned, turning my very bones to dust. "Ashes to ashes…" the fire whispered in the vampire's ear.

I placed my palm in the center of his chest. One second later, he was aflame. He screamed in agony, but though I still straddled him, the flames didn't hurt me. I watched in awe—and not a little horror—as they danced along my skin, leaving it unmarred.

And then I knelt alone on a pile of ash. Deep inside, the darkness laughed and a tiny crimson flame danced. There was nothing I could have done to stop it. But the scariest thing of all?

I'm not sure I would have.

Chapter Eighteen

I don't remember how I got back to the hotel. One minute I was on that dark street kneeling in a pile of ash, and the next I was standing in the hotel lobby with the ubiquitous Francois fussing over me.

"Mademoiselle Bailey! Where have you been? Mademoiselle Jones has been *most* upset! Most upset. Is everything OK? You look most distressed!" He talked at about ninety miles an hour, arms waving in the air. Every other sentence came out an exclamation. Honestly, he was exhausting, and I was exhausted enough already. The weariness was soul deep.

"I'm fine, Francois. My meeting just went a bit longer than I expected."

"But Mademoiselle—"

"I'm fine," I cut him off, voice firm. "Good night, Francois."

He was still muttering and wringing his hands when I turned my back on him and headed for the elevator.

Inside, I slumped against the wall. I tried desperately to dredge up any memory of the trip back to the hotel, but no matter how hard I tried, it was a no-go. The last thing I could remember was Bob doing a great ash-pile impersonation.

I knew I hadn't fought off the darkness—or the fire, for that matter. I'd had zero control. They'd let me go.

"Shit." I ran a hand through my hair and realized it was shaking. I was not doing my reputation as a vampire hunter any good. I stepped off the elevator and headed for Kabita's room.

The door swung open at my knock. "What on earth happened to you? You look like you've been rolling around in a dustbin."

"Pretty much," I said, stepping past her into the room. "I dusted Bob."

"Who?"

"The vamp that killed me three years ago."

Kabita sat down abruptly on the edge of the bed. Her mouth worked as though she was trying to say something but couldn't quite figure out what. Finally, "His name was Bob?" She sounded incredulous.

"Not exactly. He didn't tell me his name, so I figured I'd give him one."

She smirked. "So, what happened?"

I leaned my butt against her desk and crossed my arms over my chest, projecting a calm casualness I didn't feel. "We had a chat. I dusted him. Simple as that. One thing, though. He said someone hired him to follow me around. You know what that means?"

She frowned. "It was a hit. No way he'd just follow you and not try to kill you again once he learned you survived. Nothing pisses a vamp off like learning a kill didn't die."

"Or in this case did, but lived to tell the tale," I pointed out.

"Why would someone want to kill you? Other than the fact you're annoying, of course." She leaned back, crossing one leg over the other, and gave me a cool look.

I very maturely stuck out my tongue. "I have no idea in this particular instance. He said the woman's name was Jade."

Kabita sat up abruptly. "Did you say Jade?"

"Uh, yeah. Why?"

She hurried over to the desk and riffled through some paperwork. "I had a little chat with Simone Williams today. She didn't know anything, but she did have an e-mail Dara sent her after she disappeared. Adam traced the IP address. I did a little digging.

Here." She waved some sort of official-looking document at me. "Jade Vincent. Otherwise known as Dara Boyd."

I snatched the paper from her. "No frigging way. Bob said the Jade who hired him was a hunter, but not like me."

"Obviously the same Jade. I don't imagine there's another Jade who is also a hunter running around."

I scanned the document. It was an application for Miami University for a girl named Jade Vincent from Miami. The age was right, but that didn't mean anything. Dara Boyd had last been seen in London. Miami is a long way away. "How do you know this is Dara?"

She sighed and handed me another piece of paper. This one was a phone bill for one Alister Jones for the year Dara Boyd had disappeared. One number had been highlighted several times.

"What's this?"

"The phone number for a man named William Rhodes. My father called that number numerous times right before Dara Boyd disappeared. Then afterward? Nothing. Not a single phone call."

"What does that have to do with Dara? Who is Rhodes?"

"William Rhodes was head of the agency responsible at the time for witness relocation. They were friends. My father often visited the Rhodes home—in Miami." Her voice was grim. "William Rhodes has a sister named Ann Vincent. Jade Vincent is her adopted daughter. My father circumvented MI8 and all the safeguards to hide a dangerous woman in another country. And now she's back."

"And she wants me dead."

"Apparently."

"Fantastic." This really wasn't my day.

"What did Sandra's friend have to say?"

I sighed and flopped down onto the bed Kabita had vacated. I quickly told her about Julia's diary and what Drago had told me, including the fact that the dragons hadn't made Jade Vincent, aka

Dara Boyd. I knew she'd figure out the connotations of that all on her own.

"Drago's fairly certain that whoever let the dragon hunter loose and murdered Julia is trying to start a race war between humans and dragons again, most likely in an attempt at genocide. Gods, can this day get any better?" You could have cut my sarcasm with a knife.

Kabita didn't say anything. She just swung open the minibar and took out a tiny bottle of tequila. The liquor disappeared in one swallow. "You want something?" She waved at the rest of the selection.

"Hell, yes. Make it a double."

∽

I sat on the edge of my bed staring at the photograph I kept in my wallet. It was late and I needed sleep, but after the events of the day, I felt the need to ground myself, and so I sat staring at my father like somehow I could reach into the past and unlock it.

My mom had given me the photo on my twelfth birthday. I've always known my father died when I was a baby, but Mom never talked about it.

She talked about *him* plenty. How brave he was, how strong and smart. When I was being particularly stubborn, she'd tell me I was just like him. It always made me proud to be told that. Even when it wasn't exactly a compliment.

Then she'd given me the photo when I was twelve. Probably because I'd nagged her to death with questions about him. It was the first time I'd ever seen his face. Mom said it was the only one she had of him, but it was right for me to have it. Since then, I've kept it close, but hidden out of sight. It is the one thing I have of my father, and I don't want to share it with anyone.

In the photo, Dad was standing next to another man, slightly older. Dad was young, maybe twenty-five, with wavy brown hair and one of those ridiculous mustaches popular back in the seventies. Still, he was a handsome guy, and confidence oozed out of every pore, even in the photograph.

Around his neck hung a medallion on a short cord. I've always thought it looks pretty cool, that medallion. It is a starburst sun with the rays in wavy lines. No idea what it means, but I've always felt like I should know it. Like it is connected to me in a way.

But as I stared at the photo, it wasn't my father who drew my eye. It was the man standing next to him. The man with the thick, dark hair and the neatly trimmed sideburns, but the graininess of the old technology and the wear on the photo made his face somewhat indistinct. Still, something niggled at the back of my brain.

I frowned at the photo, wondering why the stranger felt so familiar. And then it struck me. It was beyond bizarre, but I was sure I was right. I'd bet anything the other man in the photo was Kabita's father.

Why was my father in a picture with Alister Jones? And why hadn't Alister said anything about knowing my father? For that matter, why hadn't Kabita ever mentioned that our fathers knew each other?

My jaw grew tight, and I rolled my shoulders to try to release some tension. Somehow I needed to find out, though I doubted Alister would ever tell the truth. Maybe Mom knew something. I'd never thought to ask before. Then again, I'd never met Alister Jones before. Perhaps Kabita would know.

A pounding on my door drew me out of my reverie, so I laid the photo on the desk and went to answer it. I sighed when I saw who it was. "Trevor Daly. What the heck are you doing here?" I turned back to the room, assuming he'd follow.

"I thought you might want to know Jack's gone." A wry smile spread across his handsome face. "He caught a flight this morning. He asked me to give you this, figured you wouldn't be interested in seeing him."

"He got that right." I took the note from him and stalked toward the desk to turn on the kettle. I suddenly felt the need for a hot chocolate. Or maybe a coffee. Something, anything. I was feeling a bit frazzled. "Funny he's OK leaving me alone now, though. He's been such a pain in my ass about this guardian crap."

Trevor shrugged. "Maybe he thinks you're safe enough with me and Kabita."

I gave him a look. "Jack would never consider anyone better at the protection thing than he is."

Trevor smiled at that. "I'm not an SRA agent for nothing. I've got some tricks up my sleeve."

"I bet."

I opened the envelope and scanned the contents of the note:

Morgan,

I'm sorry for everything. I will always care for you and I know you want more, but I can't give it.

I have to go, but you'll be in good hands with Kabita and Trevor.
Jack

The stilted awkwardness of his note left me cold. That was it? After everything we'd been through together?

I fussed with the chocolate makings as I tried to get my emotions under control, managing to drop a spoon on the floor. Trevor leaned over to pick it up. As he snatched the spoon off the carpet, a chain swung out of the open top of his button-down shirt. I froze.

The medallion swinging from the silver chain was identical to the one my father was wearing in the photograph.

I reached out and grabbed it so quickly he didn't have time to move. "Where did you get this?" I snarled.

"It was given to me." He tried to place his hand over mine, but I snatched it away. He was hiding something. I could tell.

"That's my father's medallion. What the hell are you doing with it?"

He swallowed. "Listen, Morgan—"

"Don't you 'Listen, Morgan' me." My voice rose. "I want to know what you're doing with that medallion, and I want to know *now*." I knew I was acting like a spoiled teenager, but I couldn't stop myself.

"It was a gift." I could feel the tension radiating off his body.

"Who gave it to you?"

He hesitated for a moment, as though considering his next move. Finally, he said, "Your father."

I swallowed. Hard. "Liar," I meant it to be loud and forceful, but it came out barely a whisper. "My father is dead."

His expression softened. "I know, Morgan." This time he did place his hand over mine, and even though I tried to shrug him off, he held on. "He gave it to me before he died."

I shook my head. "That's impossible. He died when I was a baby. You couldn't have been much older than that. Why would my father give you a gold medallion? That's ridiculous."

"I'm sorry, Morgan. This isn't how I wanted to tell you." Trevor's voice was a little strained, his mocha-latte skin glistening with a fine sheen of sweat. He was obviously nervous, which was kind of freaking me out.

Anger surged through me so hard and fast it nearly knocked me over. "Tell me the truth, Trevor. Now!"

He hesitated. I could almost see the internal battle waging.

"Your father didn't die when you were a baby."

My heart stopped. Then it started hammering so fast I thought I might pass out. "What are you talking about? Of course he did." My mom had told me so, and she wouldn't lie about something like that. "He was a salesman, and he died in a car accident."

He shook his head. "No, the sales job? That was something he told your mother because he couldn't tell her the truth. And his death? That was a lie too. To protect her, and you. He worked for the government. For the Supernatural Regulatory Agency, just like I do. He died, but not until years later. He was investigating something he shouldn't have, and he got too close." A muscle flexed in his jaw.

"Did you kill him, Trevor?" I didn't know why that thought crossed my mind, but I had to be sure. If he had anything to do with my father's death…

"Not me, Morgan." He squeezed my hand as if willing me to understand. But I didn't understand. I didn't understand any of it. "The government had him killed. He was too dangerous. They thought he was too dangerous."

The government killed my father? Shock warred with confusion. *How could they do such a thing?*

I looked down at the photo of my father standing side by side with Alister Jones. "Why? Why did they think he was dangerous?"

"Partly because of the investigation and partly…" He hesitated.

I looked up. Whatever he saw in my face pushed him forward.

"And partly because he wasn't entirely human."

If he'd expected me to be surprised, he was disappointed. I already knew the freaky weirdness about my DNA. My Atlantean genes had to come from somewhere.

I gave Trevor a good hard look. He works for them—for the government that killed my father. It didn't matter that his hand hadn't held the knife or the gun or whatever they'd used. It mattered that he works for an agency that kills people just because their DNA isn't entirely human.

Of course, the argument could be made that I do the same, but I don't. I kill the monsters that prey on humanity. I do not kill innocents.

My right hand clenched into a fist. "So, I guess that means I'm a threat too, huh? Daughter of a nonhuman. I guess that puts a price on my head, then, seeing as how I work for the same government." Probably not the best idea to taunt a government agent, but what the heck.

His voice was so quiet that I almost didn't hear. "Well, then I'm a monster too, and there's a death price on my head."

It took a moment for his words to sink in, and even then, I wasn't sure I understood what he was saying. Wasn't sure I grasped the entire picture. "What did you say?"

His chocolate-brown eyes stared directly into my mossy-green ones. "He was my father too, Morgan."

"Get the fuck out." I searched his face, his features, but there was nothing familiar. Nothing like mine. I was sure of it. "You're a liar." It came out a lot less confident than I was aiming for.

"No. I'm not. And you know it." He pulled the cord up and flashed the medallion. "This is the sun symbol of the Atlantean royal bloodline passed down from father to son for generations. I'm your brother, Morgan."

As though from a distance, I watched him take my hand, his dark skin a sharp contrast to my pale skin. For the first time, I realized we had the same shaped hands. Hands like my father's. Like our father's.

With that strange sixth sense I have, I knew in my gut he was telling the truth.

My brother. Trevor Daly is my brother.

I needed something a lot stronger than hot chocolate.

I let go of his hand and backed away. It was all too much, and I was starting to feel overwhelmed—panicky, even—but before I could say anything, my cell phone rang.

"Yeah?"

"Morgan, I think I'm in trouble."

"Inigo? What's wrong?"

There was a crackling on the other end of the line. "I'm being stalked. Someone wants me dead."

"Shit. What happened? Where are you?"

"I'm at home. I'm safe for now, but, Morgan, hurry. Please! There isn't much time."

The phone went dead.

Chapter Nineteen

The flight home was just this side of a nightmare. My whole body thrummed with eagerness to *do* something, while my mind was consumed with worry about Inigo.

Inigo, who'd once kissed me senseless. Who'd once told me he loved me.

There's always been a sort of light flirtation between us, but nothing more than that. He is Kabita's cousin and much too young for me. And then there'd been that kiss, followed by some strange supernatural reaction, and I'd blacked out. After that, things have been...awkward between us.

It had only gotten more awkward when he told me he loved me. Because even though I was kind of thrilled to hear it after crushing on him so long, I was already with Jack. It was too late.

Or was it?

Seriously, I was going to drive myself batshit crazy if I didn't get my mind off Inigo. There was nothing I could do until we landed. And once I kicked the ass of whoever was causing him trouble, then we could talk about...stuff.

I slid a look at Trevor out of the corner of my eye. Kabita was stretched out on one of the sofas trying to take a nap, though I could see her entire body humming with worry over Inigo.

Trevor had opted to sit across from me. The good thing about flying in a private jet was that we could have a decent conversation without anyone overhearing.

I hadn't told Kabita yet about Trevor and me. It was all too weird, and I was trying to get used to the idea before I told anyone else, even my best friend. Still, she had that look that told me she knew something was going on, for all that she was focused on the situation with Inigo.

A low chuckle escaped him. "You don't have to be subtle, you know. If you want to stare, go ahead. We're family, remember."

Family. Until now, family had been my mom, my grandma, and various aunts, uncles, and cousins. My dad had been a bedtime story, and siblings hadn't even factored into things. Now I had a brother. A freaking brother.

Dear gods. My mother was going to blow a gasket.

"Why didn't you tell me all this before?"

"The time never seemed right. And for a long time, you were just another hunter. You were safe. All that's changed now."

"What do you mean, all that's changed?"

He gave me a look that was not unlike the one Kabita gives me when she thinks I am being obtuse. "You think I don't know what Jack is? And with the crap that's going on with MI8...It was time."

It made sense. "Um, so obviously we don't have the same mom." I winced. *Way to go, Captain Obvious.*

Fortunately, Trevor appeared to have something of a sense of humor, after all. "No. My mother's name is Anita. She married our father when she was just eighteen. Dad was twenty. They married because she was pregnant."

"With you?"

He nodded. "Yes. I'm an only child." He glanced at me. "Was an only child. You can imagine the scandal at the time, an interracial couple pregnant out of wedlock. It wasn't easy for either of them."

"No, I imagine it wasn't. Did they love each other?"

He gave me a smile that held a hint of sadness and maybe a little pity. I ignored the pity. "Yeah, they did. They were crazy about each other—at least for a while. Then Dad discovered what he was."

I cleared my throat. "The Atlantean gene?"

He nodded. "Not just that, but the royal bloodline. His dad was ill, dying, so he gave him the medallion along with the story. That's how it's done."

Would have been nice if someone had bothered to tell me the story. I made a mental note to ask Jack why he'd never told me about it.

"So, what happened? How did he meet my mom? I mean, I know how they met. They ran into each other in a grocery store, literally."

He grinned. "Yeah, Dad told me about that."

I was surprised. "He did?" I couldn't imagine a man telling his son about the other woman in his life. Then again, what I know about my dad could fill a thimble.

"Yeah, he told me a lot of things." He leaned back in his chair, hands folded over his stomach. I could tell the memories were making him sad, but I needed to know. "I think he knew they were going to kill him, that it was only a matter of time. So he passed the medallion to me when I was fifteen.

"He told me about your mom then. How he was sent to Portland on a mission. How they met, fell in love. By then my parents' marriage had fallen apart. They barely spoke to each other. It was…" He shook his head.

I didn't know what to say. I was so used to being on my own, the whole family-solidarity thing was beyond me. I had nothing in the way of comfort to offer him.

He shook his head as though to clear it. "It was love at first sight with your mom. She got pregnant with you right away. I don't know what he planned to do, if he planned to leave us or what. In the end, it didn't matter."

"Why?" I frowned.

He turned his head and looked me straight in the eye. "Because the minute he found out your mother was pregnant, he knew what you were."

I was truly baffled over that one. "What does that mean?"

"Morgan, I have a single Atlantean lineage from the royal bloodline passed to me through my father. You, however, have two bloodlines, both royal."

"Excuse me?"

169

"Your mother is Atlantean too."

I gaped at him, mouth open like a fish. "Are you nuts? My mother? The woman who obsesses over my love life and spends her time playing gin rummy with my grandmother?"

"That's the one." He grinned.

"Does she know?"

He shook his head. "Not at all."

I mulled that one over for a moment. Yeah, my mother would definitely freak over the whole Atlantean thing. She has no idea the supernatural exist, never mind our family's special connection to ancient mythology. "How does she not know? That she's of the royal bloodline? How could my dad not have known earlier?"

"Dad knew. It just didn't really matter one way or the other until your mom got pregnant. As for your mom, well...You know your mother better than I do. But I'm guessing this is not the sort of information she needs to know about."

"No kidding," I said with some fervor.

He laughed. It was good to see him smiling. Damn, why was I all protective of him all of a sudden?

"Anyway, he'd kept his life with your mom carefully hidden from the agency, but when she got pregnant, he had to leave you in order to keep you safe. He thought it was the only way to keep certain elements in the government from finding out about you. He did a damn good job of it too. They never knew he had a second child.

"After he left, he had a friend contact your mother telling her he'd been killed in a car accident."

"What about his body?" I couldn't imagine my mother just accepting that the man she loved was dead without proof.

"The excuse was a car fire. She didn't accept it at first, but eventually..." He shrugged.

Eventually, she would have had to get on with life. She had me, after all. And I'd bet Dad's friend had been persuasive.

"He went back to my mother. Tried to make it work. They had several more years of being miserable together," Trevor continued. "He never regretted it, either. Hiding my lineage was one thing; he faked the tests so it looked like I hadn't inherited the gene, but hiding yours was another thing altogether. Especially with your hunter abilities, though they were latent."

"What do you mean? I got my abilities from the vampire attack."

"No, you didn't," Trevor said. "You always had them. The attack only unlocked them."

Holy shit. "I was born a hunter?"

"More or less."

I wasn't entirely sure what to do with that information. Or, for that matter, whether it made any difference. I decided to mull it over later. Avoidance, thy name is Morgan. I decided to ask an easier question.

"What about dragon hunters? I thought they were made. Why the difference?"

"Simple. Vampires and demons and such are predators of humanity, so evolution came up with a natural counterbalance— the hunter. Dragons, however, were never our natural enemy, and therefore, nature had no answer."

"But Alister Jones said that in ancient times dragons used humans for food," I said.

"Alister Jones wouldn't know the truth if it bit him on the ass."

Interesting. And it certainly made sense.

"But surely they know about you, the government? If they knew about Dad. They must have retested you when you joined."

He shook his head. "Of course they did, but one of Dad's friends from back in the day owed him a favor. He was able to swap out my test results with some faked ones."

"Didn't they know because of your name?"

"Daly is my mother's maiden name and I use it, so on a day-to-day basis most people at the agency don't realize who my father was. Didn't your mother ever tell you Dad's name?"

"No. She left it blank on my birth certificate. She just always called him my dad, and when I asked? Well, you think *I'm* stubborn." I come by that gene honestly.

He nodded. "Maybe he asked her to do that to keep you both safe. Or maybe she just didn't want to talk about him."

"Yeah, that sounds like her. So what was his name?"

"Alexander Morgan."

I swallowed hard. "Mom named me after Dad?"

The smile on his face was warm and genuine. "Yeah. She did. Dad told me that too."

"Why did he tell you about me? Surely he must have known it would upset you to know he'd loved someone besides your mother. That he had this whole other family out there." I knew it hurt me, even though part of me was thrilled to know I had a brother.

"I guess it did, at first." He tilted his head back, thoughtful. "But one day, when you were really little, Dad took me by a park. You were there with your grandma. You were so little, so precious. Dad told me you'd need me. That someday I'd need to find you, protect you. He made me promise. So that's what I did. I joined the agency under my mother's name so I could use their records to find you, and when I did, I made sure I was put in charge of your team."

I blinked back tears. All this time he'd been watching out for me as best as he could. "But why? Why have you been protecting me?"

He shook his head. "I can't explain why. Just…Since that day in the park, it was like you were mine. I was your big brother, and it was my job. I know it sounds a little nuts, but it was something Dad asked me to do."

"Not any more nuts than most of the other things that have been happening lately." I tucked my hands back in my lap. "This is weird. Sorry, but I'm sort of…wigged out a little. I mean, it's cool. I always wanted a brother, but…"

"But this isn't quite how you pictured it?" His grin was wry.

"No, not exactly." I grinned back.

"That's OK. You'll get used to it. We both will. I'm not going anywhere."

I honestly had no idea how I felt about that. I mean, the idea of having a brother was kind of cool, but on the other hand, I was finding out things about myself that made me doubt everything I'd ever known. I felt confused and, I admit, a little betrayed. By my father, my mother, and Trevor. Gods, things were screwed up.

I decided it was time to change the subject. I'd had enough crazy family talk, and the situation with Inigo was still gnawing at me. "So, do you have any idea what's happening with Inigo? You are the government man extraordinaire, after all." I knew I came off a bit flippant, but I was really worried. I'd tried to ring Inigo several times before we took off, but no luck. It kept going straight to voice mail. I couldn't seem to help the edge of panic lurking inside me at the thought of his being in danger.

"I think it has to do with his heritage."

"Excuse me? How does being English put him in danger? It's not like we're at war or anything."

He sighed. "There's more to it than that." He glanced over at Kabita, who appeared asleep. But looks can be deceiving. "You really need to speak with Kabita."

"If it's about his clairvoyance, I already know about that."

"Like I said, you really should talk to Kabita. It's her secret, not mine."

That just made me more worried. And a little mad. What hadn't they told me? What could possibly have put Inigo in danger? I could only hope we weren't too late.

I squeezed my eyes closed. If we were too late, I didn't think I could bear it.

∽

Inigo's place was a wreck. My heart sank to the floor, and if Kabita's expression was anything to go by, hers did the same. To say the signs weren't good was an understatement. There'd been an almighty fight, and it was pretty clear Inigo hadn't been the victor.

The thought drove my earlier discussion with Trevor right out of my head. All I could think about was the fact that Inigo might be hurt. Or worse.

Trevor had dropped us off before heading to a meeting with a confidential informant. He wouldn't say anything more specific than that, but I figured it had something to do with Inigo and tried not to get annoyed. I like things clear and up front. And no, the irony of that statement, in light of the things I was hiding from my best friend and my new brother, is not lost on me.

Kabita prowled the living room, her face a mask. I could feel the anger rolling off her in waves, but underneath the anger were fear and anxiety. And something else—she blamed herself.

"This wasn't your fault, Kabita."

"I should have been here, protecting him. Not off playing detective. I was in the shower and didn't even answer when he called." She picked up a picture frame and carefully swept the shattered glass away from the photo inside. It was a picture of the three of us taken the day Kabita opened the detective agency. We all had cheesy grins and big glasses of champagne.

Inigo had insisted on champagne even though I didn't like it. He'd said a celebration without champagne was like cake without chocolate. That had been a good day.

Gently, I took the photo out of her hands and placed it on the mantel. I'd buy him a new frame. "What kind of trouble is he in?" My voice was quiet, but firm. It was time for answers, and the only way I could get past the terror of Inigo being hurt was to face this head-on. Calmly and logically. Like Mr. Spock.

"It's hard to say." She sighed. "Inigo is...different. Some people don't like different. Some people exploit different."

I assumed she was talking about his clairvoyance. There are plenty who'd be happy to exploit that, though it seemed strange they'd go to such extremes. Why not just hire him?

I opened my mouth to ask, but something under the edge of a couch cushion caught my eye and I crouched down. On the floor, underneath the cushion, was a stain. The coppery scent hit my nose. Blood.

"Kabita."

The minute she spotted the blood, her expression turned even grimmer, if that were possible. She clenched her fists until her knuckles turned white. "Oh, Goddess."

"Hey." I reached over and squeezed her arm. "We don't know this is his blood. He could have hurt his attacker. Besides, there isn't enough blood for whoever's it is to be truly hurt." I refused to let my own fear show in my face.

My cell rang. Trevor. "Yeah."

"Just had a meeting with my informant. If anyone on the streets knows anything, they aren't talking. I'm sorry, Morgan."

"Hey, you did the best you could." It was more than I'd expected him to do. "But something definitely went down here. The place has been trashed."

"My CI promised to keep an ear out. If she hears anything, I'll let you know."

"Thanks." I hung up and relayed the information to Kabita.

"I guess that leaves one option," she said. "Get a map."

"For what?" I couldn't imagine.

"I'm going to try to scry him."

I stared around the room vaguely, as if a map might suddenly jump out at me. Maps are a little archaic nowadays, and not something I generally carry around with me.

"Uh, how about this?" I pulled up a map application on my phone. The streets of Portland popped up on the screen.

"Never tried to scry with a cell phone app before. This oughta be interesting." She lifted her necklace from around her neck and wrapped the cord around her hand, leaving just a few inches for the pendant to swing free. The pendant itself was a small chunk of raw rose quartz. "Zoom out as far as you can."

I zoomed out until the map showed the whole of Portland with pretty much zero detail. Kabita held the quartz over the screen of my cell phone and closed her eyes. The crystal started swinging gently, then stopped, the tip pointing toward downtown.

"OK, zoom in a bit," she said.

I adjusted the map until it showed downtown. This time the crystal pointed to Chinatown.

Kabita repeated the process until the crystal finally pointed to the old Hung Far Low building. The Chinese restaurant was once famous throughout Portland for its rather creative name but is now just an empty shell.

"There might still be time." I dialed Trevor. "We've got a location." I gave him the address.

"I'm headed there now. Be there in five."

"OK, we're on the way, but we'll be a bit longer," I told him.

"I'll check things out while I wait for you. If I need to, I'm going in," he said.

"Good. Turn your phone on vibrate. I'll text when we get there." I hung up the phone and turned to Kabita. "Trevor's on his way."

Her face flooded with relief. "Good. We need all the help we can get."

I had no doubt of that. As I headed toward the car, I felt the darkness swirl inside me, wanting out. The darkness had enjoyed dusting Bob the vamp, and it wanted to kill whoever took Inigo. It enjoys killing, period.

What scares me is that when the darkness is in control, I enjoy it too.

I pushed that thought aside. I didn't have time for introspection.

I pointed the car toward downtown and pressed down hard on the accelerator, barely making it through a yellow light. I turned left onto Burnside, which spit us out into downtown. To the left lay Chinatown and the former home of Hung Far Low. I turned up Fourth Street and found a place to park not far from the former restaurant.

I sent Trevor a quick text. An instant later, he responded, and Kabita and I hustled down the block to meet him.

"Is he in there?" Kabita demanded.

"I have no idea. There aren't any windows, and I didn't have a chance to go inside. I don't like doing this without backup, but they're still twenty minutes out. But if he is in there and he's alive, we need to go in now." His gun was already out.

I don't carry weapons deadly to humans—other than my blades, that is. A little flame sparked inside me, reminding me I carry one weapon deadly to everyone but myself. I damped it down. The fire isn't for humans, either, as far as I am concerned. I don't care what it wants.

Instead, I slid my dagger from its sheath. There'd been no time to head home from the airport, so that was the best I had.

I glanced over at Kabita. She had a gun too. *Damn, where'd these people get guns all of a sudden?*

Trevor moved to the door, which swung open quietly. I raised a questioning eyebrow.

"Already picked it," he explained in a hushed voice.

I wasn't entirely sure that was legal, even if he is an SRA agent. But frankly, I didn't care. All I could think about was getting to Inigo as quickly as possible.

We stepped through the door into what had once been a large dining room. It was empty now, save for a broken chair sagging against one wall and a crappy poster with curling corners lying on the floor.

"Kitchen," Trevor hissed.

Fortunately, the kitchen doors were those swinging kind with the little round portholes. I peered through, and my heart froze. Inigo was next to the stove, his arms stretched up above his head, chained to a support beam in the ceiling. Additional lengths of heavy chain wrapped around his ankles and were padlocked to the stove.

He sagged against the chains, his face bruised and swollen, hair matted with blood. I gasped in horror as a young woman with short blonde hair whispered something in his ear, then hauled off with a baseball bat and hit him in the stomach. Inigo doubled over, or at a least as far over as the chains would let him.

Trevor had to hold me down. I wanted to rip that door off its hinges, storm into the room, and rip the person who'd hurt Inigo into little bitty pieces.

"Wait, Morgan, we need to go together." Trevor kept his voice low in my ear. "And someone needs to block that back way."

"She's going to kill him." In fact, I was surprised he wasn't dead already. I had to fight to keep the tears out of my voice. "That bitch is going to kill him if we don't stop her *now*." I didn't know how any human being could survive a blow like that.

"I'll go block the back." Kabita's whispered voice was colder and harder than I'd ever heard it, her face grim with determination. In her eyes, I saw murder and wondered if she could see the same in mine. Inigo is ours. And we protect what is ours.

Trevor gave her a brief nod, and she disappeared out the front door. It would take her a moment to get around back, so we had to wait. Meanwhile, the bitch inside was going at him with that bat. Worse, I could hear her laughing.

Seriously, she was going to die.

My palms burned with heat, and I struggled to shove the fire back down. It didn't want to go; it wanted out, and if I were honest, I wanted to let it out.

"You OK?" Concern laced Trevor's voice. I must have looked like a crazy person.

"No." I hissed, trying to keep my voice low. "I'm done waiting."

Chapter Twenty

I burst into the kitchen, Trevor hot on my tail. The girl wheeled around, dropping the bat and pulling out a gun so quickly it made my eyes go wonky. She was too fast for a human. Then my brain caught up with me. She obviously wasn't entirely human.

"Federal agent. You are under arrest. Drop your weapon," Trevor shouted from behind me.

The girl sneered. "Drop yours, *agent*." She said *agent* like it was a dirty word. "I'm faster than you could ever hope to be."

Without warning, the darkness roared through me, and everything funneled down to Inigo and the girl. One second I was standing next to Trevor; the next I was across the kitchen with my knife at her throat. "You're not faster than me," I snarled.

Swifter than the eye could see, she had the gun pressed to my temple. *Shit. Not good.*

With a heave, the darkness surged up out of me, and in that moment, I let it go completely. Hell, I embraced it. The darkness reached out with my hand and slapped her hand back, sending the gun flying. With a shriek of rage, she was on me, her own knife drawn.

We went down in a tangle of limbs and blades. She was small, but she was strong. Really strong. Stronger than me, except for one thing—the darkness evened the odds.

Somewhere in the background I could hear Trevor yelling. The darkness ignored him. So did I.

I grabbed the girl by the throat and flipped her over, smashing her head against the floor—hard. If she'd been an ordinary human, she'd have been dead. As it was, it stunned her long enough for me to snap her wrist. Her knife fell with a clank to the floor. She screamed with pain, but it didn't stop her from grappling for my knife.

Using her legs for leverage, she flipped us both over so she was on top, digging into my knife arm with her good hand. I threw a punch at her face with my left hand, but she saw my fist coming and dodged. Her hand pressed harder on mine, bringing the knife closer and closer to my throat, and I suddenly realized I'd underestimated her. She was a hell of a lot stronger than I'd thought.

The darkness screamed in anger, and for a moment, I pushed back harder, but the angle was wrong. I couldn't get the leverage I needed. The blade kept coming closer.

Trevor was suddenly there shouting at her to let me go. His gun was pointed straight at her, but she ignored it. Instead, she kicked out with one leg so fast it was a blur. Trevor went flying across the kitchen.

Panic surged through my body as I struggled to keep the blade away. This girl had a power unlike any I'd ever seen before. I suddenly realized that, darkness or not, there was no way I was winning this fight.

Unless I was willing to let loose the fire.

"Stop right now, bitch, or I'll blow your head off." Kabita's voice was stone cold. Her gun was pressed up nice and tight against the back of the girl's head.

The blonde froze, but her eyes still burned with hatred. Slowly, she raised her hands. Kabita kept the barrel of the gun pressed firmly against the girl's head, but let her get up off me. The fire had other ideas.

With a snarl, I flipped the girl back under me. My right hand burned. I glanced down to find it glowing white hot, fingers cherry red. Fire danced at the tips of my fingers. I glanced back at the girl and raised my hand. The sneer left her face, and for the first time, she looked truly afraid. I lowered my hand toward her chest as the fire roared inside me.

"Morgan, stop!" Inigo's voice, slightly ragged from his ordeal, cut through the haze in my head. I glanced at him, confused. "Morgan, we need her. OK? You have to stop."

I hesitated, my hand inches from the girl, struggling to pull the fire back. Little black dots danced in front of my eyes, and I felt myself growing a little woozy. Blacking out was not an option.

I glanced back down at the girl under me. She stared back, hatred written across her face. Inigo was right; we needed her. With sheer force of will, I pulled the fire back inside me. The glow in my hand dimmed to orange, then red, and finally turned normal, the fire slowly receding, leaving behind utter exhaustion. But I couldn't collapse. I couldn't let the girl see my weakness.

I glanced back up. Kabita was getting Inigo out of the chains, and Trevor was snapping special SRA handcuffs onto the girl's wrists. I staggered to my feet, dazed with exhaustion. I felt like I'd just woken from a dream; everything felt so out of focus and confused.

I ignored Trevor and his prisoner and headed over to where Inigo had sunk to the floor. I was pretty sure the only thing holding him up was the stove. Kabita had found a first aid kit somewhere and was trying to clean him up.

The sight of him injured nearly undid me. I wanted nothing more than to break down and cry, but I swallowed the lump in my throat.

"Here, let me." I knelt beside them and took the kit from her. She gave me a strange look, but nodded and moved back. I pulled an antiseptic pad from the kit with shaking hands and gently swiped it over a cut above his eye. He hissed as the medicine went to work cleansing the wound. "Are you OK?"

Stupid-ass question. There were chain-shaped burn marks on his wrists and across his throat. How had she done that to him?

"I'll survive." His voice was rough. "She didn't do any damage that won't heal."

"You need a doctor..."

"I'm fine." His voice was firm.

I clenched my jaw. I didn't care what he said; he needed a freaking doctor. Sooner rather than later.

"Why was she after you?"

He shook his head slightly. "I have no idea. She wasn't interested in talking. She was more interested in..." He nodded toward the bloody bat and chains.

I swallowed back bile. "How'd she get you in the first place?" I knew from experience that Inigo was not an easy person to sneak up on.

"She's a hunter."

"I'm a hunter, and I can't sneak up on you like that."

"She's different." He caught my eye and gave me a look as though willing me to understand. "Her skill set is different than yours. She's a dragon hunter."

I whirled and gave the girl a hard look. For the first time, I realized I knew her. "Jade?"

Her head snapped up. "How do you know my name?"

Kabita stood up and stalked toward her, leaving me to finish fixing up Inigo. "You're Jade Vincent, originally named Dara Boyd. Born in London, England. Disappeared five years ago."

"My name is Jade," she hissed between clenched teeth. "As far as I am concerned, Dara Boyd is dead."

"Fine. Jade." Kabita squatted down to her eye level. "You know Alister Jones."

She shrugged. "Yes. He's my godfather."

Kabita and I exchanged looks. Kabita obviously hadn't known about this godfather business. Must have been part of Alister's cover for Jade.

I nodded. "He sent you to live with the Vincents as soon as you turned eighteen."

Jade cocked her head. "Yeah, how'd you know?"

My turn to shrug. "I have my ways. So, tell me, Jade, why'd you go back to London? Let me guess. You wanted to help out your godfather, Alister."

She smirked.

A lightbulb went off. "You killed Julia Reynolds."

Jade settled herself more comfortably on the dirty floor, though I couldn't imagine it was too comfortable with her hands cuffed behind her back. "Bravo. Got it in one."

Her sheer arrogance astounded me. She actually sounded proud of the murder.

"Why?"

She tilted her chin up. "It's what I do."

"There's more to it than that."

She gave me an appraising look. "Julia knew too much. And when she started poking around asking questions, she had to go."

"What sorts of questions?"

She shrugged. "Little favors I did for my godfather."

My guess was those little favors involved murder. "So Alister brought you out of hiding to take care of his problem. Cover his ass." Fury was riding me, but I beat it back. I needed to think clearly. "How did you do it? Slice her open like that?" It would have taken some doing to mimic a dragon claw. Not to mention some serious cojones to toss her entrails around.

"Trade secret."

The bitch just smiled at me. Gods, how I wanted to slap that smug look off her face.

"Why did you frame the dragons?" Trevor interrupted.

She gave him a bland look. "Hello! It wasn't Julia's fault she had to die. Her death shouldn't be without meaning. What better way to die than to die serving your country and bringing down our enemies, restoring MI8 to its rightful place?"

It made sense. In a psychopathic nut job kind of way. While the other agencies carried on officially, MI8 languished in obscurity. So part of it, at least, was Alister's driving need for power. He wanted MI8 back at the top of the intelligence food chain. Unfettered by ethics and laws. A race war with the dragons would do that, hurried along by the fears of a nation. Fears fueled by lies.

I shuddered at the thought of it. If Alister had accomplished his mission, he'd have no doubt been given complete power over all the supernatural races. Gods knew what Alister would do with that kind of power, but I'd bet my life it was nothing good.

"Dragons are evil," Jade hissed at me. "They need to be destroyed before they destroy us."

"Did Alister tell you that?" Inigo snarled. "The dragons have been the guardians of humankind, not the enemy. That's Alister's twisted reality, not the truth."

Something slid through Jade Vincent's eyes. Something not quite human and very definitely crazy.

"The stories are true, then." My voice was quiet. "Without the rogues to hunt, the dragon hunters went insane."

"We were bred to kill dragons," she hissed. "And we will not rest until every last dragon is dead."

"Yet you are the last of the dragon hunters. It's over, Jade," Inigo said. I could tell from his expression he thought that was a good thing. I didn't disagree.

"It's never over. Alister will finish what we started."

Trevor gave her a grim smile. "Alister's days are numbered. He won't be in power for much longer. MI8 has discovered a number of his illegal activities. Even as we speak, the authorities are moving in."

Kabita was lounging against the stove, her body language less tense now that we'd found Inigo. She nodded. "Dex has been appointed lead investigator. He'll do what's necessary."

I glanced over at Kabita, wondering how she felt about all this. Her dad is essentially a traitor to the crown and her brother had been forced to turn on him. It had to be rough, but Kabita was keeping her emotions very close. I couldn't get a read on her.

"Good." I turned back to Jade. "What about Bob?"

"Bob?" She gave me a blank look.

"The vampire. The one that killed me three years ago? And that other one that attacked me in Hyde Park?"

"Oh." Her laughter was a light tinkle, so at odds with her bag full of crazy. "That was just a distraction. Alister told me about your run-in with…Bob. I figured they'd keep you busy or kill you. Either way worked for me. It would keep her out of my hair." She nodded at Kabita. "Plus, I figured if anyone could track me, it would be another hunter." She gave me a scalding look. "Never figured you were so slow."

I ignored the insult. "What about Inigo?" I demanded. "Why him?"

Her laugh held an edge of wildness. "God, you're thick, aren't you? Just like Alister said. We were going to use him to call out the dragons, but then Julia got her nose stuck in where it didn't belong and we had to kill her."

"Use Inigo to call out the dragons? How? Why?"

Before Jade could answer, Kabita interrupted. "Why did you take Julia's heart?"

The thing that had clued me in. The thing that didn't fit. I found it hard to believe that, after all that planning, Jade had screw up so phenomenally.

"What are you? Some kind of idiot? When a hunter eats the heart of her prey, she takes on the prey's power. It's an honor."

186

It was so bizarre it took a few seconds for it to click. *Ew. Gross.* I was pretty sure my face mirrored the look of horror on Kabita's.

Jade frowned. "Her death was supposed to stir up fear, blah, blah. But it didn't work, thanks to you getting your nose into everyone's business and trying to protect those stupid beasts. So I had to go back to the original plan with him." She nodded at Inigo. "But before I could do that, I had to deal with you." She shook her head as though I'd personally insulted her by being difficult.

"I still don't understand what this has to do with Inigo." I tried to get my brain back on track. Erase the horrific image she'd put in my mind.

"He had to die just like the others. Inigo Jones is a freaking dragon."

I froze. *What the fuck? Is she insane?*

But something clicked in my mind: the extra body heat, the smell of s'mores, the golden eyes. I shook my head. It was just so damned ridiculous.

"OK, fine, you don't want to answer me. Whatever."

"I think it's time I take the bitch to jail," Trevor interjected. "I've got a special cell picked out for her."

Naturally, he meant Area 51. It's where the SRA detains all their "special guests."

Trevor's backup had finally arrived, and they hustled Jade out to a waiting van. The thing looked more like an armored truck than any sort of regular transport. It made me feel better somehow. The crazy bitch was going away for good.

Trevor and I hugged each other and said a quick good-bye before he hopped into the front seat and headed out with his team. He didn't say anything about meeting up, but I figured we'd see each other soon enough. I headed back over to check on Inigo.

"What, you guys are all cozy all of a sudden?" Kabita sounded less than pleased as she glanced from the departing vehicle to me. Apparently, Trevor's help hadn't appeased her one iota.

"Yeah, well, we sort of have to get along now. He's my brother."

Two pairs of eyes, one set blue and one brown, stared at me like I'd just grown a second head.

"Excuse me? Did you say Trevor Daly is your brother?" Kabita said.

I could hardly blame them for their shock.

"Listen, I'll tell you both all about it later, but I think we've got bigger things to worry about." Like loony-tunes Jade and whatever Alister had planned.

My hands roamed over Inigo, checking his injuries. "Are you sure you're going to be all right?"

"Yeah." He gave me a slight smile. "I'll be fine."

"Damn, am I glad you're OK." I gave him a big hug. Nearly losing him made me realize that he means more to me than I'd wanted to admit. I couldn't imagine not having him in my life, and I knew he'd never hurt me. Whatever this thing between us was, we'd figure it out later.

"Easy." His breath was warm against my ear. "I just got beat up by a girl."

I smiled and snuggled into the warmth of him. Gods, he smelled good. Like campfires and autumn and hot chocolate.

My mind stuttered to a halt, remembering the smell of Drago. He, too, had smelled of campfires and chocolate. The similarity in their scents was undeniable. My brain simply didn't want to deal with how those numbers stacked up. Coincidence. Had to be.

Except, Jade had said Inigo was a dragon. And while she might be nuts, she was still a dragon hunter.

Oh, gods.

"That poor girl really did go nuts, huh?" My words were muffled against Inigo's chest, his arms still wrapped around me as if he wasn't quite ready to let me go. I didn't mind.

"What do you mean?" His voice was a little rough.

I pulled back a little. "Oh, come on. That crack about you being a dragon?" I waited, praying he'd tell me what I wanted to hear. That it was a mix-up. A joke. Anything but the truth I feared it was.

He and Kabita exchanged a look. "Yeah, it was a pretty stupid comment."

"See." I tried to snuggled back in, but his next words froze me into place.

"I'm only half-dragon."

∽

I scooted back out of Inigo's arms and staggered to my feet, my gaze dodging wildly between him and Kabita. "Stop messing with me."

He pulled himself up too, using the stove as a crutch. "I'm telling you the truth. My father was a dragon. My mother was human. I am a halfling."

My eyes wide, I searched his face. He seemed sincere, but it was all too mad. I couldn't even take it in. I think maybe I'd had one too many revelations lately. I turned to Kabita.

"It's true."

I shook my head. "You said he was your cousin."

"He is. Of a sort. My many times great-grandfather had a sister. She was raped by a rogue dragon in human form. When Inigo was born, it was clear that he wasn't entirely human. It was also clear she had to hide his true nature."

"I don't understand."

"Dragons kill halflings." Inigo's voice was hard. "Especially those sired by rogues. We are considered impure and a threat to the continuation of the race. My mother and her family hid me from the dragons. They've been protecting me ever since."

189

I was trying really hard not to hyperventilate, but it was all too much. "How…um…How old are you?" Gods, this was like Jack all over again, only worse. At least I'd known what Jack is from the beginning.

"Only four hundred years."

"Four hundred." It came out a mere squeak.

"I'm sorry that I lied to you, Morgan." Kabita stepped toward me. "But I had to. As Inigo's protector, I was sworn to secrecy. As was each protector before me. To keep him safe from the dragons, everyone had to believe he was human. That's my job. I didn't want you in danger. And knowing the truth would have put you in danger."

I swallowed hard. The truth was that I did believe them. I just didn't want to. "Too late. I'm already in danger most of the time. How did Alister find out?"

"He's always known. He's family," Kabita said. "Obviously, he was just biding his time until he could use our secret."

And he had—to try to start a war.

Inigo heaved a deep sigh. "It's time, Kabita."

"No…"

"Yes. She means too much to me to keep her in the dark any longer. She needs to see the truth for herself."

Her face was strained, but she nodded. "I'll give you some space."

I just stood, feeling sick to my stomach, as she exited the kitchen. My best friend had been lying to me for three years. Inigo had been lying to me. Gods, I didn't know which was worse. I completely ignored the fact that I'd been lying to them too.

He reached out and cupped my face in his hands. "Morgan." His voice was warm and smoky and held just a hint of pleading. It wrapped around my heart, begging me to understand. "I've wanted to tell you for so long. Since the moment I set eyes on you, I've wanted you to know who I really am. What I really am."

His pupils slowly elongated, his irises morphing from blue to gold. I sucked in a breath. I'd seen those eyes before.

"That night. The one I can't remember. Your eyes did that." We'd fought vampires together that night, and then we'd kissed for the very first time. It had been amazing right up to the moment when I blacked out. I remembered nothing after that kiss, and I had to admit it kind of freaked me out a little.

"Yeah." His voice was a sigh. "I can usually control the shift, but something about you...I can't always control myself." His laugh held an edge of wildness.

I swallowed hard. "Do you remember that night? What we did?"

He leaned his forehead against mine, and the world went away. It was just the two of us wrapped in the scent of campfires and hot chocolate and the gold glow of Inigo's eyes. "No," he whispered. "I wish I did, but I don't. I remember nothing after the kiss." His lips brushed mine, velvety soft. "After that, all I remember is heat. Then darkness. Then nothing at all."

"So you don't know if we..." My voice trailed off. I wasn't sure what I wanted the answer to be.

He shook his head. "I don't know. I hope we didn't. I want to remember our first time together."

I swallowed. "Yeah, me too."

His thumbs caressed my cheeks, his breath warm as he touched his lips to mine. "Stand back and watch carefully."

I did as he told me. I felt cold without his warmth, so I wrapped my arms around myself. My mind was having trouble grasping the situation. All I felt was confused. Then hard on the confusion came hurt and a little bit of anger that he hadn't trusted me to keep his secret safe.

But I soon forgot my upset as I watched as Inigo's skin began to shimmer and glow, turning a golden hue. His body shifted, elongated, the glow growing brighter and brighter until it hurt my eyes. Then, suddenly, in the middle of that dingy kitchen stood a dragon the size of a large horse. My mouth dropped open. Surreal didn't begin to cover it.

He looked exactly like the dragons in fairy-tale books, with a long, spiked tail and wings kind of like a giant bat. Except that Inigo's wings were cerulean dusted with gold and looked as soft as brushed silk. His scales were similar to the one I still had in my pocket. Only, his had the rich blue, green, and purple hues of New Zealand abalone.

He was incredibly beautiful.

"You can touch me if you want." Inigo's voice jarred me out of my shock. Except, I wasn't hearing him with my ears; his voice was inside my head. *"I don't much like people touching me, but you're different."*

I admit to being a little nervous as I approached him. He brought his head down to my eye level, his gold eyes boring into mine. "Hey." It came out a little croaky, and I swear I saw him smile.

He gave me a gentle head butt, so I reached out and stroked my hand down his side. His scales were smooth and hard, but suppler than the one I had. That made sense. Like skin, which is soft and elastic when alive, but grows hard and tough when dead.

He butted me again, and a laugh escaped me. I rubbed his nose, which was surprisingly soft, and he let out a sound that was very close to a purr. "You really are beautiful," I whispered to him, all my anger and hurt and confusion forgotten. "I wish you'd shown me sooner."

My hand gently brushed his wing. It was softer than silk, unbelievably so. I ran my fingers over it again. He shuddered and rubbed his cheek against me.

"I've dreamed of this, you know."

I caught Inigo's face between my palms, leaning my forehead against his, much as he'd done to me earlier. "What do you mean?"

"I've been in love with you since the day I met you."

You know how in romance novels they always talk about hearts singing? Well, that was what I felt like. I cleared my throat, beating back a blush. "Is that so?"

He huffed.

I laughed. "Of course it is, and I know it. I've always known it, haven't I? I've just been too stubborn to admit it." A thousand butterflies were going crazy in my stomach. "I...I think I'm in love with you too."

"There's nothing I've wanted more than to show you my true self. To have you accept me for who I am. All that I am."

I nodded. My throat was so tight I couldn't speak. My heart was thumping hard against my ribs, and I was afraid I might cry. Everything was just so overwhelming.

I cleared my throat, but my voice was still a little wobbly. "I take it your clairvoyance comes from being a dragon."

He nodded his big dragon head. *"Yes. Along with the ability to manipulate human minds. It's a dragon thing. With you, it seems to go a bit wonky, like you're partially immune or something. I think that's what happened...that night we were together."*

I felt myself flushing again and pressed my cheek tighter against Inigo's smooth scales. He made a little grumbling sound but didn't pull away.

"So, now you know the truth, the whole truth."

"Trevor knows?"

"Yes, he had to. He's the liaison between the dragons and the US government. Not that he's ever had to do much. No one's heard from them for years until now. Still, he figured it out."

"That's what he's got on you and Kabita." I'd caught Trevor blackmailing Kabita into a job a couple weeks back, only I hadn't known at the time what he had on her.

"Yeah."

"Sounds like Trevor and I need to have a talk."

"He's just doing his job, Morgan. Don't go all ninja on his ass."

I snorted. "I'll try to restrain myself." I stroked Inigo's nose again. "Can you change back?"

He stared at me out of golden eyes, then slowly nodded his head. He nudged me a little, and I stepped back. This time I watched the shimmer with interest and fascination. It was really kind of cool. Pretty too.

The shimmering stopped, and Inigo stood there in human form, still wearing the clothes he'd been wearing when he shifted. Apparently, the clothes went with his human form. I couldn't help myself. I walked over, wrapped my arms around his neck, and kissed him. There were definitely tongues involved.

"Ah, Morgan, I'm sorry," he said when we finally came up for air. "I wanted to tell you. I wanted—"

"Shh." And I kissed him again. Best way to shut up a man, ever.

Chapter Twenty-One

All right, so why didn't you just shift and go all dragon on the crazy bi—" I broke off as Kabita glared at me. Not a fan of the B-word, Kabita. "Uh, the crazy lady." We were headed to the car, moving slowly for Inigo's sake.

Inigo snorted with laughter. "And start another war between dragons and humans? I think not. That would have given her exactly what she wanted. Besides, she was using silver chains. I can't shift when silver is touching me."

"What, like werewolves?"

He rolled his eyes at me. "I'm nothing like a werewolf, but yes. The principle is the same."

"How'd she get a drop on you, anyway?" Kabita interjected. "I know dragon hunters can control dragons, but that wouldn't have worked with your human half."

He shrugged and wrapped his arm around my shoulders, hugging me to his side. "I knew she was tracking me, which was why I called you. No way I could fight her on my own. If I was full dragon, that'd be one thing, but I'm not strong enough. I figured I'd just stay out of her way until you got here."

"Why didn't you call the SRA?" I asked. "They could have sent someone to help."

Inigo shook his head. "The SRA doesn't know, and I don't want them to know. Trevor is the only one who does, and he was with you two in London.

"In any case, it worked for a while. But then the bi…uh… hunter got sneaky. She coated my front doorknob with nightshade extract."

I must have looked confused, because Kabita translated. "Nightshade acts as a strong sedative for dragons when they are in human form, even through the skin. It would have knocked him out in seconds."

"By the time I came to, she had me chained and a gun to my head. I tried to fight, but the chains…" He held up the burn marks on his wrists. "I don't know what she did to them, but it was like using silver on a vamp. I had no choice but to do what she said. Fortunately, I knew you wouldn't be far behind." I was glad someone had so much faith in our abilities.

"Come on, let's get out of here." Kabita climbed into the car. "This place creeps me out."

I couldn't help but laugh.

∽

I was glad to be home. Really glad. Everything was exactly as I'd left it, right down to my steampunk-style boots lying in the middle of the floor and my bed piled high with unfolded laundry.

I would have stayed at the hospital with Inigo—Kabita had finally threatened him into submission—but he'd insisted I go get some sleep. I'd given in, and good thing too. Jet lag was creeping in, and combined with the emotional roller coaster of the last few days, it was draining the energy from my body. I felt wasted. Even worse, I felt gross. Like I hadn't showered in days.

I left my suitcase in front of the bedroom door and headed for the shower. I'm sure I've said it before, but the restorative powers of a hot shower are vastly underrated.

I didn't even bother to dry my hair, though I did manage to towel off. I just staggered from the shower to my bed, shoved the laundry to the floor, and climbed in.

Lights out.

⌢

I was back on top of the wall overlooking the valley. Cold wind slapped into my face, carrying a few snowflakes with it.

"You've done well, Hunter. We are grateful."

I turned. A smile tugged at the corner of my mouth. He was in human form, his inky-black hair dancing in the wind.

The wind carried away my laugh. "Hey, Drago. I was just doing my job."

"More. You did not only your job; you also did what was right. As you promised. Justice has been served."

I shook my head, sending brilliant red strands flying. "Not enough. Not yet. Alister Jones is still in power—at least for the moment—and gods know what kind of crazy he's up to."

"'Tis true. Alister Jones has yet a part to play, but for now, he is no longer a threat."

I frowned, the light was dimming, and it was hard to see his features clearly. "What do you mean, he has a part to play?"

"You shall know soon enough. See you soon, Hunter." He opened his mouth and flame engulfed me.

⌢

"Dammit!"

The swearing followed an almighty thump that woke me from dead sleep.

What the hell? "Inigo? Is that you?" I'd know his voice anywhere.

"Who else? Did you have to leave your bloody suitcase in the middle of the bloody doorway?" His British accent was heavier than usual.

I grinned in the dark. "I figured it would discourage trespassers."

"Smart-ass." He sank down on the bed next to me.

"What are you doing out of the hospital? You're supposed to be there overnight for observation."

"With those nurses poking and prodding me every hour, I've had all the observation I can stomach."

I couldn't blame him. I remembered my own stay in the hospital after the vampire attack. I'd nearly decked one of the night nurses after she'd woken me up for the third time in one night.

"Morgan, I need to ask you about Jack."

"What about him?"

"I know the two of you had a…thing."

I almost laughed at that. *A thing.* Yeah, you could call it that. I didn't think laughter would be the best response, so instead, I just shook my head. "That's over, Inigo. Well and truly over."

I realized in that moment that I meant it. I mean, yeah, part of me still cares for Jack and probably always will, but what I feel for Inigo is so much stronger. So much…more.

"You're sure?"

I slid my hand up his thigh. "Never been more sure of anything in my life. When I knew you were in trouble…" I shook my head. I couldn't finish the thought.

His hand unerringly went to the back of my skull, digging into my hair. He tugged me gently forward.

His lips were as I remembered. Velvety soft and tasting of campfires and hot chocolate. It was a little weird, but good weird.

Heat unfurled inside me, swirling through my body into all the places I hadn't realized were so cold. My fingers dug into the softness of his T-shirt, the heat of him underneath like a living flame.

I skimmed my hands under his T-shirt so I could feel his skin. Without a second thought, I pulled it up and over his head and tossed it on the floor. My own T-shirt followed close behind.

My heart fluttered at his touch. It was a strange mix of comfort and excitement. I felt like I'd come home.

I felt his tongue flick across my nipple before he pulled it into his mouth, and pleasure speared through me, my panties growing damp from want. I arched up into him, and he grinned as he took my other nipple into his mouth.

I threaded my fingers through the silk of his hair, pulling him up so I could kiss him. Our tongues and breaths tangled together as fire surged through my veins. I went from damp to wet in a heartbeat.

Inigo moaned, his hands slipping under the waistband of my pajama pants. They found what they were looking for, his fingers slipping through my wet folds. Pleasure stabbed through me. I arched up again and made a noise low in my throat that sounded suspiciously like begging. His fingers swirled around my clit until I thought I'd come right then and there.

"Inigo," I pleaded.

He kissed me again as he slipped one finger inside me, thrusting against my sensitive flesh. The pressure built, winding me tighter and tighter. I writhed against his hand as he pushed me up and over the edge. For a second, I forgot to breathe. I let the orgasm take me.

He pulled back, and his eyes had gone gold. Like the night I couldn't remember.

"Inigo?" This time I said it with fear. I didn't want to forget.

"Shh…" He kissed me, more gently this time, as he slid his hand out of my pants. "We'll remember."

I nodded as I helped him get me first out of my pants and then him out of his jeans. Finally, we were both naked, our bodies dimly outlined by the faint moonlight. I ran my hands across his smooth chest and down his stomach, the thin line of silken hair leading down to…

"Holy gods."

He smirked a little at that, but there was pride too. Believe me, he had plenty to be proud of.

I ran my fingers lightly over the length of him. He shivered, and his eyes drifted closed, shutting off the golden glow. My fist barely closed around the thickness of him, and I gave him a quick pump. Then a second. I loved the hard, velvet feel of him.

"For the sake of all that is holy, Morgan," he hissed at me. "If I don't get inside you right this second…"

His scent hit me hard, the smoky chocolate teasing my senses and sending heat pooling between my thighs. I ached to feel him inside me.

"Then we'd better do something about that." My voice was low and breathy as I handed him a condom from my nightstand. Nothing like I usually sounded.

I lay back, pulling him down with me. I could feel the thick head of his shaft, the tip just touching my core. "Now, Inigo, I want you right now."

In one thrust, he was inside me, the thickness of him filling and stretching me almost past bearing. I grabbed his butt, holding him still for a moment so I could adjust. His jaw was clenched tight, and beads of sweat popped out on his forehead, but he held it.

Then I moved.

A slight roll of my hips and we were both goners. All I knew was the thrust of him inside me, the feel of his skin, the golden glow of his eyes, the taste of his tongue, and his smoky chocolate smell that mixed with my own arousal and wrapped around us growing stronger.

Then, in one final thrust, he sent us both over, the pleasure so intense I'm pretty sure my eyes rolled back in my head. But not before I got to see the look on Inigo's face as he came inside me.

I cherished that image as he sank down half on the mattress and half on top me, his skin slick with sweat and his heart hammering hard against my own. Our limbs still tangled together. We stayed that way until our hearts calmed, our bodies cooled, and his eyes slowly faded from gold to blue.

∽

We were still curled up naked together, my face buried against Inigo's throat. That sweet spot where the neck and shoulder meet.

I couldn't believe this was happening. Had happened. I'd wanted him for a long time, but I'd never thought we'd actually be together. Not like this. Not for real.

Part of me was so happy I could cry.

The other part of me was scared to death. What if I fucked this up? What if he left me? Like Alex.

Like Jack.

I had to distract myself, fast, before I talked myself out of something good. I pressed myself tight against him and breathed in his scent. "Mmm…You smell good."

He rubbed his cheek against my hair and gave my butt a little squeeze. "What are you talking about?"

"You smell like a campfire." I squirmed around so I could see his face better. "And chocolate."

He raised a brow. "Interesting."

"It's a dragon thing, isn't it?"

He rolled over onto his back, taking me with him so I ended up sprawled across his chest. The insecure girly part of me that still lurked somewhere inside tried to freak out that I was too heavy, that he'd see my thick thighs and chubby tummy. That he'd rethink this whole thing and tell me he couldn't do it. That he'd leave me like…

I told her to shut it.

After all, Inigo is a freaking dragon. He could take my weight. And he isn't Jack. Or Alex. "So…" I prompted.

"So, yeah. It's a dragon thing. Kind of like human pheromones, but a lot stronger. The way a dragon smells lets members of the opposite sex know whether they're compatible. Apparently, it works on humans too." He gave me a smug look.

I nipped him with my teeth. Just enough to sting.

"Hey, ow! Morgan!" But there was laughter in his voice.

I just batted my eyelashes at him and feigned innocence.

"So, every dragon smells different?" I was still thinking about Drago and how similar he smelled to Inigo.

"We all smell different, but dragons of the same sex who share a sire will have a very similar scent."

It couldn't be. Could it?

"That means if you had a brother, he might smell chocolaty too?"

He shrugged. "I guess. But I don't have a brother."

"How do you know?"

His expression grew bleak. "Because if I did, he'd have hunted me down and killed me by now. Removed the stain to his family's honor."

"That's bullshit." I'd met Drago. He didn't seem like the brother-murdering type.

"It's the way it is, Morgan. Dragons believe that halflings are a scourge. A stain on the purity and honor of the race."

I frowned. "If that's true, I don't think I like dragons very much."

He grinned at that and kissed me. Hard. "I love you, Morgan Bailey."

My heart went into overdrive. I stared at him like an idiot. The very idea both scared me to death and thrilled me to pieces.

"Um, was that a joke?" It came out a lot more whispery than I'd planned. "Or did you mean it?" He'd said it before, but somehow I hadn't really processed it until that moment.

He sat up slowly, taking me with him. His expression was grave as he gently tucked a lock of hair behind my ear.

"I mean it, Morgan. I've been in love with you forever."

I licked lips suddenly gone dry. "Why didn't you tell me then?"

"Your life was in chaos back then." His voice was low and warm, his hand gliding gently up and down my back. Soothing me. Apparently, he thought I might just go flying off the proverbial handle. He was probably right.

"You had barely survived a vampire attack. Hell, you'd actually been dead. You were training to be a hunter, moved thousands of miles, given up your life in London. Your whole life had just been turned upside down, and the last thing you wanted or needed was for some young idiot to go stomping into your heart like a bull in a china shop."

"So, you thought you'd, what, do the friend thing?"

He sighed. "I guess so. I thought I'd give you time. Time to adjust, get used to your new life. Get used to me. Except, it didn't quite work the way I'd planned."

Yeah, I'd thought he was too young for me. I guess the joke was on me. Then there'd been the Atlantis thing. And Jack, who I'd thought was "it." Not to mention that I'd thought Inigo was Kabita's cousin, and I didn't want her killing me for playing Mrs. Robinson. Which is pretty funny considering he is nearly four hundred years older than me.

"I wish you'd told me. About what you are." There was a twinge of hurt deep inside me at that. Why couldn't he have trusted me enough to tell me the truth?

He pulled me hard into his arms, nearly squeezing the breath out of me. "Anyone who knows the truth about me is in danger, and I could not risk your life like that."

I frowned, but cuddled into him anyway. "But I risk my life every day. It's what I am."

"I know. But at least, this way, it wasn't me putting you in danger."

Stupid man. I thought about being pissed off at him for a minute, then decided against it. In his thickheaded male way, he'd tried to do the right thing. I couldn't blame him for that.

I pulled back slightly and poked him in the chest with my forefinger. "From now on, I want the truth, got it? No more hiding shit from me, OK?"

"OK." His answering grin held plenty of relief. "Deal."

"Oh, and, Inigo?"

"Yeah?"

His eyes flashed with hints of gold as I leaned forward to give him a quick kiss.

"I love you too."

The first thing I saw when I woke up the next morning was a very nice male backside headed toward my bathroom. It took me a moment, but it finally registered that half that backside was covered with a very odd tattoo.

"Inigo?" I couldn't take my eyes off the tattoo.

An exact replica of his dragon form's scale pattern was tattooed in shimmering ink from his right hip, all across his right butt cheek, and down over his right thigh. It was breathtakingly beautiful but also incredibly unusual. It was the first time I'd seen it, as it was also the first time I'd seen Inigo entirely naked in daylight.

"Just going to take a quick shower. Wanna come?" He turned around and leered at me.

"You bet!" I practically flung myself out of bed. Overeager idiot. "But I was kind of wondering about your tat. It looks just like your scales."

His hand went self-consciously to his hip. "It's not a tat. It's a birthmark."

I stepped up to him, running my own hand along his hip and over his backside. His skin was just as smooth as I'd remembered. "It's the most unusual birthmark I've ever seen."

"Full dragons have the pattern all over their bodies when in human form. It mimics their scales in dragon form. They're able to hide them with glamour if they want to."

"You're not?"

He shook his head. He looked a little uncomfortable. "No. I'm a halfling, so my glamour isn't strong enough. Besides, I've only got the pattern in this one spot so..." He shrugged.

"You hide it. Well, I think it's beautiful." And I do.

The smile that broke across his face warmed my heart. Inigo may have been a four-hundred-year-old half dragon, but apparently, his heart was as vulnerable as mine. What a pair we make.

"Come on, Dragon Boy," I said, smacking him on the backside, "there's a hot shower with our names on it, and I expect you to make me come at least twice before breakfast."

He made it three.

Chapter Twenty-Two

I admit I felt ever so slightly awkward as I placed two cups of coffee on the table along with some toast and eggs. Inigo and I had finally, finally slept together. It changed everything.

"Hey." Warm hands grabbed my hips and pulled me down onto an equally warm lap. Inigo's lips met mine, lush and delicious. I sighed and leaned into him, soaking up his heat.

He pulled away slightly, his blue eyes serious. "You're right; this changes things. But it changes them for the better, OK?"

"Dammit, did you read my mind?"

He smiled. "A little."

I stared at my hands, feeling my throat grow tight and my eyes hot. I would not cry. I wouldn't. "The last time I loved someone, really loved someone, he told me he didn't love me anymore. He left me. For someone else. And when I thought I'd found someone else to love, to trust, he turned on me too. I know that's not you. I know it. But…" I hesitated. "I'm scared."

"Hey"—he wrapped his arms around me—"I'm scared too. You just saw me turn into a dragon. That's a lot to ask a girl to accept."

And just like that, I relaxed. Everything was going to be OK.

Well, maybe. I still had to tell him about the darkness and the fire.

He handled it amazingly well, although I could tell he was worried. "We'll figure it out, Morgan." He squeezed my hand. "I promise. I'm just glad it's keeping you safe."

He made a good point. It is, in a weird way. The darkness makes me stronger, faster, and harder to kill. The fire gives me a weapon like no other. Which is a good thing in my line of work. Unfortunately, my little superpowers have a serious downside. If they took over, if I lost control, things could go to hell awfully fast.

We were halfway through breakfast when the phone rang. I checked the caller ID. Kabita.

"Morning."

"Is Inigo still there?"

I could feel myself flushing bright red. "Uh, yeah, how did you know?"

"Oh, please, Morgan."

I could visualize her rolling her eyes at me. I passed the phone to Inigo.

"Yeah." There was a pause followed by a series of "uh-huhs" and "OKs" before he hung up and handed the phone back to me. "We need to fly back to the UK."

"What, like now? I just got back."

He smiled, but it was a little strained around the edges. It was pretty clear he wasn't looking forward to the trip. "There's a conclave tonight at midnight. Drago has asked for you to be there."

I got up from the table and went to wash my dishes. "A conclave?"

"Yeah." He joined me at the sink. "A conclave of dragons. It's sort of like the Senate convening. It's a rare event, but it's very important."

"Why would Drago ask for me?" Granted, he'd seemed to like me well enough—for a human. But there was a difference between finding a person amusing and inviting them to your species' most important government session.

"When Drago asks, you don't ask why. You just do it."

I turned to face him, leaning my back against the cupboard and crossing my arms over my chest. "You're going?"

"Of course."

"Why would you? What have the dragons ever done for you? They're nothing but a threat to your life."

He sighed as he curved his hands over my hips, pulling me against him. I wanted answers, but I let him wrap himself around me. I couldn't help it. I liked it too much. Inigo had always been touchy-feely, but I was seeing a whole new side of him. A side that needed both to give and receive comfort and strength. I liked it.

I ran my palms up and down his back, the heat of him soaking into me, warming me. I felt the fire inside flicker to life, but not in an angry way, like it usually does. This was more like it recognized kindred. Like it hungered for another like it. Little by little, I let it out, relieved when it stayed low. It seemed satisfied enough with Inigo's touch.

Could Inigo be the key to controlling the fire? After all, Fina's best friend had been a dragon. Perhaps there was more to that. I filed that little tidbit away for future examination.

"Humans were a threat too. Back then, people were afraid of what they didn't understand. Hell, they're still afraid of what they don't understand. But four hundred years ago, that could get you dead."

"And the dragons? Would they still try to kill you?"

He shrugged and stepped back a little. The fire didn't like it and tried to flare up, but I coaxed it down. Either I was getting better with this whole control thing or Inigo's presence really did have a calming effect on it.

"I don't know. Most likely. Halflings have been under a death sentence since ancient times. Granted, the dragons have been off the grid for centuries, but I don't see that their edicts would have changed much."

I frowned. "Humans have changed. Why wouldn't dragons?"

"Dragons can live for millennia. They tend to take the long view of things. Change comes a lot more slowly."

"Fine." I nodded. "I'll fly over with Kabita, and you can stay here. Now that Jade's locked up, you should be safe enough. Alister can't possibly have another dragon hunter up his sleeve. Though I don't know how they expect us to make it by midnight. It's six p.m. over there, and it'll take at least fifteen hours."

He shook his head, blond hair catching the morning sunlight and turning to molten gold. "Kabita's not going. She's going to be coordinating Alister's takedown with MI8 in London. I'm going with you."

"Oh, hell no. If there's a death sentence for halflings, I'm not letting you anywhere near the dragons."

"Kabita assures me Drago has promised safe passage. Dragons do not give their word lightly."

I still didn't think it was a great idea. If things went wrong, he'd have to go into hiding again, this time even deeper. "But I thought they didn't know about you."

"Apparently, they do now." His jaw clenched. He was clearly not happy about that. "Besides, I'm not just going with you; I'm taking you."

"Taking me?"

He grinned, and this time it was the old cocky Inigo. "Yeah, I'm a dragon, remember? I can fly a lot faster than a seven forty-seven."

I swallowed hard. "You expect me to fly on your back all the way to London?"

"Nope." He laughed, scooping me up off my feet like I weighed nothing and hauling me toward the bedroom. "You're going to ride on my back all the way to Hadrian's Wall."

$$\infty$$

If watching Inigo shift from his human form into his dragon form had been cool, riding a flying dragon from Portland to the northern edge of England was a hundred times cooler. And I wasn't just talking about the temperature, though believe me, that was plenty cold. Thank goodness for Inigo's higher-than-normal body temperature.

Inigo had shown me a sort of complicated saddle thing, which I'd had to put on him while he was in dragon form. It was made of soft, supple leather and a padded cushion, and essentially involved me tying myself onto his back, closing my eyes, and praying to every god in the pantheon that I wouldn't plummet to earth and die a horrible death.

The terrain flashed by beneath us so fast it was almost a blur. There was no way I could have survived such speed without some sort of tinkering with the laws of physics.

As we flew, I realized that while he was too busy concentrating to speak to my mind, I could feel what Inigo was feeling. I could feel the thrill of flying, the joy of having me on his back.

Alongside that were the physical sensations: the cold wind against my face, the smooth scales under my palms. I could feel Inigo's heat and the vibration of his flight even through the saddle. The sensations were incredibly erotic.

I wondered if he could feel what I was feeling the same way I sensed his emotions. The answer that came was a resounding *Yes!*

A laugh burst from my throat. I forgot my fear and gave myself over to the pure joy of flying through the night on the back of my lover.

Inigo was right. Dragons, even half dragons, can fly a heck of a lot faster than a 747. I don't know how he did it without killing me in the process, but we made it just in time. Midnight struck as my feet touched the top of Hadrian's Wall.

Moonlight bathed the wall and the valley below, coating everything in shades of silver. I gazed around and sucked in a breath. On every side were the hulking shapes of dragons quietly watching me out of glowing golden eyes. I held back a shiver.

Inigo, still in dragon form, nudged me gently from behind. I felt a sudden wave of warmth and security and realized he was using his mental gifts to give me courage. I rubbed his forehead, grateful for the support, though most of my fear was for him.

"So, Halfling, you debase yourself to a mortal, allow yourself to be treated as a brainless farm animal." The low, grumbling voice was familiar.

"Hello, Drago." My voice was just ever so slightly tart. It wouldn't pay to piss off the king of dragons, but I wasn't about to let him insult my boyfriend. Lover. Whatever. I had no idea what to call Inigo, but I knew he was mine. "Is this the sort of hospitality I can expect from your kind?"

He was in human form, but I swear he suddenly grew bigger. "Pardon?"

"I am your guest, here at your behest, and yet you insult me."

"Insult I may have given, but it was not meant for you, Morgan Bailey."

"And yet your very implication that I am less than your equal is an insult. Not to mention that any insult to Inigo is an insult to me. Remember, it was a mere human who saved your asses." He could stick that in his pipe and smoke it.

Drago inclined his head, his bearing regal. "The point is well taken, Morgan Bailey. I beg pardon for the insult to you and your...friend."

"Thank you. Apology accepted." I turned to Inigo. "You should go now. You can pick me up later." I wanted him out of there and away from the threat of the other dragons. Despite Drago's promise that Inigo would be safe, I didn't trust that he wouldn't be hurt somehow.

"There is no need," Drago spoke up. "He is perfectly safe here."

I raised both brows at that. "From what I hear, you have a penchant for murdering halflings."

Drago snorted at that, a little wisp of smoke escaping his nostrils. "It has been many human generations since we ceased such barbaric practices. Even without my promised safe passage, he would never come to harm among us."

Inigo's eyes widened. "Excuse me?"

Drago looked amused. "We aren't in the habit of killing our own kind."

"But halflings—" Inigo started.

Drago let out a sound of exasperation. "Halflings are dragon kin," he said as if that finished the matter.

I believed him. Or, to be more accurate, the fire inside me believed him. It knew he told the truth the way I know when a vampire is near. I could see that Inigo was in shock, and I didn't blame him. Four hundred years of hiding, and for what?

I turned to the matter at hand in order to give him a little time to recover. "May I ask why I have been invited to your conclave?"

"Of course." Drago smiled and took my arm, eliciting a tiny grumble from Inigo.

I shot Inigo an annoyed look over my shoulder and he quieted. He was always so easygoing until it came to me.

"First, let me introduce you to my other guests." Drago drew me farther down the wall to where two human men stood. I knew them both immediately. "These are the liaisons between my people and yours. Dexter Jones and Trevor Daly. Gentlemen, this is Morgan Bailey."

They nodded politely, and I followed suit, though I was somewhat surprised to see Dex. I started to open my mouth, but Trevor gave his head a little shake. I guess that meant they'd arrested Alister, but apparently, we were keeping our cards close to our chests. I wasn't sure why, if we were all friends, but then, I've never been too good with political bullshit, so what did I know?

I stepped away from Drago to shake hands first with my brother, then with Kabita's brother. As we shook, Dex whispered, "Dad got wind of the investigation and disappeared."

"Shit."

"No kidding," he sounded tired.

"So you're in charge?"

"Yeah. Not that I wanted this."

I squeezed his hand. "That's why you'll be so good at it."

"Hope you're right."

"And you, of course, know our dear friend." Drago turned me slightly to face the large oak that grew up from the center of the wall. A woman wrapped in a white cloak stepped from the shadows.

"Sandra!"

She smiled her winsome smile. "Hello, Morgan. Lovely to see you again. I'm so glad you could make it."

"Yeah, great. Now, will someone please be so kind as to tell me why I'm here?" I've never had much patience, and what little I had was rapidly running thin.

"We invited you here," Drago said, "to honor you, Morgan."

I turned to him, surprised. "Honor me? Why?"

"Two reasons. First and foremost, by your faith and your action, you have saved our people from genocide at the hands of a madman."

I wasn't sure about the madman part. Alister Jones had seemed frightfully sane. "And second?"

"Second..." His mouth curled into a smile and his campfire-s'mores scent curled around me as he placed his right palm over my heart. The heat was intense, and before I could stop it, the fire inside me rushed out, across his hand and up his arm.

"We honor you, Morgan Bailey"—his voice boomed across the valley—"as fire bringer."

Hundreds of dragons launched themselves into the air, fire gushing from their mouths. The shrieks and cries were deafening, but I could only stand and stare, my mind completely numb, as the fire within me engulfed the king of the dragons.

∽

"You OK?" Trevor plopped down beside me, dangling his long legs over the wall.

"I just set a man on fire. So, no. Not OK."

"He's a dragon, Morgan. He's not just any dragon; he's Drago. He didn't burn."

I glared at him. "Like that's supposed to make me feel any better? It creeps me out even more."

Which was true. The fire that had come from inside me to engulf Drago had left him completely unharmed. In fact, he'd seemed to enjoy it. Which hadn't pleased Inigo terribly much, not that I could blame him. It hadn't exactly pleased me, either.

Apparently, according to Sandra, tradition indicates that a fire bringer is property of the Drago. And not just any property. Sexual property. Like that is going to happen. I don't care if he does smell like a frigging s'more.

Trevor took my hand. It felt good to have a brother. "Hey, at least things are looking up. With Dex the head of MI8, the edict against witches has been rescinded."

I brightened at that. "They're giving Ben his job back?"

He laughed. "Ben Landry is now a very rich man. Julia left him everything."

"Awesome." I was really glad things were turning out well for Ben. Though losing Julia probably wasn't something he'd ever get over.

"He pretty much told MI8 where to stick it. He's opening up his own consulting firm and charging triple for his services. Dex is annoyed, but Ben's one of the best techs there is, so he's going to have to grin and bear it, thanks to Alister."

"Excuse me, Mr. Daly. Might I have a word with Morgan?" Sandra's musical voice broke into my thoughts.

"Of course, Ms. Fuentes." He stood and gave my shoulder a squeeze. I was definitely starting to get used to this whole big-brother thing.

Sandra took his place in a flurry of robes. She should have looked ridiculous, but instead, she looked wonderfully ethereal. I had a feeling she'd spent a lot of time living between two worlds.

"So, you and the halfling, hmm?"

I clenched my fist, anger coursing through me. How dare everyone treat him like some kind of freak? "His name is Inigo."

"Yes, of course. I do apologize. I meant no offense." She drew her knees up under her chin and let out a sigh. "That's simply what the dragons call them. I forget sometimes that humans are more sensitive about such things."

It didn't escape me that Sandra didn't refer to herself as human. "What? About insults?"

She gave me a surprised look. "It's not an insult, Morgan."

I gave her a look of sheer disbelief. "Halflings are under order of execution—or they were, anyway. How can it be anything but an insult?"

Her eyes grew wide. "Execution? Oh, my dear girl. Halfling children are treasured just as dearly as dragon children. They are no less; they are equal."

"But Inigo's family, they had to protect him..." Except that the truth was that the dragons had never known about him.

She shook her head. "Old laws, ancient traditions. You can't blame them. How would they know? Humans and dragons haven't mixed in over a millennium."

I didn't know whether to laugh or cry. All this wasted time hiding. An entire family giving up their lives to protect their own.

For nothing. Inigo hadn't needed protecting. He would have been a cherished member of his clan.

"Gods. That's batshit crazy."

"Indeed. But I think everything will turn out all right in the end. Things have a way of working out the way they're supposed to."

I wasn't sure that I had her faith. But I hoped for Inigo's sake she was right. I wanted him to have some peace about his past, about his family. He deserved that.

"By the way, I'm not Drago's property," I blurted. "I don't care what the hell they said at that ceremony."

"You mean the fire bringer thing?" She looked surprised. "Of course not. That's just another one of the old ways. Fire bringer is an honorary title now. Very revered by the clans, but nothing more."

"What is it?" It was obviously a major honor, from the way the dragons were acting, but I didn't really know what it meant. At first, I'd flipped out when they started talking about me being property. Who wouldn't? But when they'd assured me it was an honor and I wasn't really his property—it was just some kind of honorary historical thing—I'd gone along with it, bowing and thanking everyone.

"Put your hand in mine. Palm up." She held out her hand, so I did as she asked. "Now, watch," she said softly.

As I watched, the center of my palm began to glow orange; then flames danced just above, swirling into a circular pattern. I could feel the fire inside me being pulled up through my hand ever so gently, but it was as though someone else controlled it.

"This is the fire that now lives inside you." Her voice was low, rhythmic.

I felt my eyelids grow heavy and my eyes lose focus as I stared into the swirling flames dancing above the palm of my hand. Sandra's voice was hypnotic, pulling me deeper and deeper.

"Millennia ago," she continued, "the tribes of man first met with the dragon clans. Surprised by their wit and intelligence, the clans swore never to harm the tribes of man. To cement their new friendship, the drago of the clans gifted one of the humans with the ability to channel fire.

"This human was called fire bringer by the clans, though her people called her a fire mage. She became the drago's lover and the intermediary between the clans and the tribes of man. Her presence could soothe even the raging anger of a dragon."

Somewhere in a distant corner of my brain, I remembered Eddie telling me about the fire mages. "Atlantis," I whispered.

"Yes." Sandra's voice stayed low and even. "The first fire bringer was of Atlantis, and every fire bringer thereafter was one of her descendants. But the fire bringers began mating with ordinary humans, and each generation grew less powerful, until one day there were no more fire bringers. Thus was born the first rogue."

I frowned. Drago had told me a little of the rogues. My mind tried to grab hold and connect the dots, but the flames above my palm brightened and swirled, and I was dragged under again.

"Without a fire bringer, the clans could not ease the troubled mind of the rogue, not even with the help of a dragon child. And so thousands of humans died.

"Over the centuries, with the ability to create fire bringers lost, dragons have gone rogue in greater and greater numbers. And without the dragon hunters, the drago has been forced to kill his own time and again, something that is anathema to the dragon race. The only chance for survival of the race was to find another fire bringer. You, Morgan, are the last human able to channel fire. And so you are the fire bringer."

She sat back and released my hand. Suddenly, I could think again.

"But no one created me. How do I have this ability?"

"No one created me, either," she said with a slight smile. "It is in our genetic code, passed down through the centuries from an ancestor who *was* created with this power."

"So, I'm some kind of peacemaker?"

"For dragons, yes. Now that you've infused the drago with your fire, the effect will trickle down to all the clans. Hopefully, it will prevent future rogues. At least for a while. In the human world, it is only a weapon."

Yeah, I had that figured out already. *Crap.* Could my life get any more complicated?

"So, he doesn't expect me to, uh, you know..."

She laughed. "I think his wife might have something to say about that."

I blinked. "He's married? Then why does he keep doing that scent thing?"

She raised a brow. "Well, he *is* the drago. It's a power display."

"Men," I huffed.

She just laughed.

We were quiet for a moment, our eyes on the dark valley. A few dragons still wheeled against the night sky, the occasional spit of fire giving away their presence.

"It's weird, though. Inigo and Drago smell a lot alike."

Both brows went up this time. "Are you sure? The human sense of smell isn't as keen as a dragon's."

I didn't bother to remind her that I was a little more than an ordinary human, fire bringer business aside. "I'm sure."

"Oh dear." She sighed. "That can only mean one thing."

I glanced over at her. I knew exactly what she was thinking. "Should we tell them?"

We both turned to look at Inigo, still in dragon form, and Drago in his human form. They were doing the male staring-contest thing. The testosterone could have killed an elephant at forty paces.

"Oh, hell no!" we both said at the same time. Then we laughed.

Sometimes it is better to let the boys figure things out for themselves.

"You know, Alister Jones is still out there, free to do this all over again," she said quietly.

Freaking fantastic. "I know. Dex told me."

She gave me a long look. Finally, she spoke, and her words sent chills racing through me.

"So, Fire Bringer, what are you going to do about it?"

Acknowledgments

Thanks as ever to my fabulous critique partners Lois and Tamra, and to my beta reader, Bonnie. The butt kicking was worth it, don't you think?

And thanks to my dad, who said, "Why can't dragons have a conclave at midnight on Hadrian's Wall?" Why not, indeed.

Don't miss Morgan Bailey's debut in *Kissed by Darkness*!

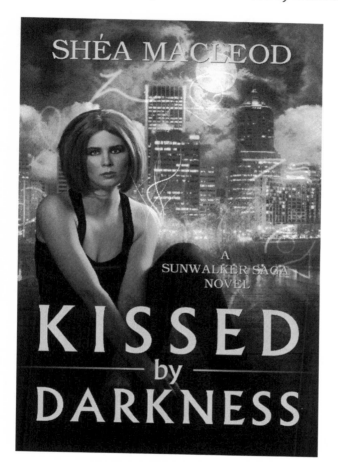

Available now on Amazon.com

About the Author

Photo by Razzaq Digital, 2012

Shéa MacLeod spent most of her life in Portland, Oregon, before moving to an Edwardian townhouse in London located just a stone's throw from a local cemetery. Such a unique locale probably explains a lot about her penchant for urban fantasy post-apocalyptic sci-fi paranormal romances, but at least the neighbors are quiet. Alas, the dearth of good doughnuts in London drove her back across the pond to the land of her birth. She is the author of the Sunwalker Saga and Dragon Wars series.

Made in the USA
Charleston, SC
28 September 2012